ELEPHANT

Also by Raymond Carver

Fiction

Put Yourself in My Shoes
Furious Seasons
Will You Please Be Quiet, Please?
What We Talk about when We Talk about Love
Cathedral
Where I'm Calling From

Poetry

Near Klamath
Winter Insomnia
At Night the Salmon Move
Where Water Comes Together with Other Water
Ultramarine
In a Marine Light

Prose and Poetry

Fires

RAYMOND CARVER

ELEPHANT
and other stories

COLLINS HARVILL
8 Grafton Street, London W1
1988

William Collins Sons & Co. Ltd
London · Glasgow · Sydney · Auckland
Toronto · Johannesburg

BRITISH LIBRARY CATALOGUING IN PUBLICATION DATA

Carver, Raymond
Elephant and other stories.
I. Title
813'.54[F]

ISBN 0 – 00 – 271912–6

Grateful acknowledgement is made to the editors of the *New Yorker*
("Boxes", "Whoever Was Using This Bed", "Elephant", "Blackbird Pie"
and "Errand"), *Esquire* ("Intimacy") and *Granta* ("Menudo") in whose
publications the stories in this volume first appeared.

First published in Great Britain by Collins Harvill 1988
Reprinted 1989
© Raymond Carver 1986, 1987, 1988

Photoset in Linotron Bembo by
Rowland Phototypesetting Ltd, Bury St Edmunds, Suffolk
Printed and bound in Great Britain by
Hartnolls Limited, Bodmin, Cornwall.

Tess Gallagher

We can never know what to want, because, living only one life, we can neither compare it with our previous lives nor perfect it in our lives to come.

MILAN KUNDERA,
The Unbearable Lightness of Being

Contents

Boxes

My mother is packed and ready to move. But Sunday afternoon, at the last minute, she calls and says for us to come eat with her. "My icebox is defrosting," she tells me. "I have to fry up this chicken before it rots." She says we should bring our own plates and some knives and forks. She's packed most of her dishes and kitchen things. "Come on and eat with me one last time," she says. "You and Jill."

I hang up the phone and stand at the window for a minute longer, wishing I could figure this thing out. But I can't. So finally I turn to Jill and say, "Let's go to my mother's for a goodbye meal."

Jill is at the table with a Sears catalogue in front of her, trying to find us some curtains. But she's been listening. She makes a face. "Do we have to?" she says. She bends down the corner of a page and closes the catalogue. She sighs. "God, we been over there to eat two or three times in this last month alone. Is she ever actually going to leave?"

Jill always says what's on her mind. She's thirty-five years old, wears her hair short, and grooms dogs for a living. Before she became a groomer, something she likes, she used to be a housewife and mother. Then all hell broke loose. Her two children were kidnapped by her first husband and taken to live in Australia. Her second husband, who drank, left her with a broken eardrum before he drove their car through a bridge into the Elwha River. He didn't have life insurance, not to mention property-damage insurance. Jill had to borrow money to bury him, and then – can you beat it? – she was presented with a bill for the bridge repair. Plus, she had her own medical bills. She can tell this story now. She's bounced back. But she has run out of patience with my mother. I've run out of patience, too. But I don't see my options.

"She's leaving day after tomorrow," I say. "Hey, Jill, don't do any favours. Do you want to come with me or not?" I tell her it doesn't matter to me one way or the other. I'll say she has a migraine. It's not like I've never told a lie before.

"I'm coming," she says. And like that she gets up and goes into the bathroom, where she likes to pout.

We've been together since last August, about the time my mother picked to move up here to Longview from California. Jill tried to make the best of it. But my mother pulling into town just when we were trying to get our act together was nothing either of us had bargained for. Jill said it reminded her of the situation with her first husband's mother. "She was a clinger," Jill said. "You know what I mean? I thought I was going to suffocate."

It's fair to say that my mother sees Jill as an intruder. As far as she's concerned, Jill is just another girl in a series of girls who have appeared in my life since my wife left me. Someone, to her mind, likely to take away affection, attention, maybe even some money that might otherwise come to her. But someone deserving of respect? No way. I remember – how can I forget it? – she called my wife a whore before we were married, and then called her a whore fifteen years later, after she left me for someone else.

Jill and my mother act friendly enough when they find themselves together. They hug each other when they say hello or goodbye. They talk about shopping specials. But Jill still dreads the time she has to spend in my mother's company. She claims my mother bums her out. She says my mother is negative about everything and everybody and ought to find an outlet, like other people in her age bracket. Crocheting, maybe, or card games at the Senior Citizens Centre, or else going to church. Something, anyway, so that she'll leave us in peace. But my mother had her own way of solving things. She announced she was moving back to California. The hell with everything and everybody in this town. What a place to live! She wouldn't continue to live in this town if they gave her the place and six more like it.

Within a day or two of deciding to move, she'd packed her things into boxes. That was last January. Or maybe it was February. Anyway, last winter sometime. Now it's the end of June. Boxes have been sitting around inside her house for months. You have to walk around them or step over them to get from one room to another. This is no way for anyone's mother to live.

After a while, ten minutes or so, Jill comes out of the bathroom. I've found a roach and am trying to smoke that and drink a bottle of ginger ale while I watch one of the neighbours change the oil in his car. Jill doesn't look at me. Instead, she goes into the kitchen and puts some plates and utensils into a paper sack. But when she comes back through the living room I stand up, and we hug each other. Jill says, "It's OK." What's OK, I wonder. As far as I can see, nothing's OK. But she holds me and keeps patting my shoulder. I can smell the pet shampoo on her. She comes home from work wearing the stuff. It's everywhere. Even when we're in bed together. She gives me a final pat. Then we go out to the car and drive across town to my mother's.

I like where I live. I didn't when I first moved here. There was nothing to do at night and I was lonely. Then I met Jill. Pretty soon, after a few weeks, she brought her things over and started living with me. We didn't set any long-term goals. We were happy and we had a life together. We told each other we'd finally got lucky. But my mother didn't have anything going in her life. So she wrote me and said she'd decided on moving here. I wrote her back and said I didn't think it was such a good idea. The weather's terrible in the winter, I said. They're building a prison a few miles from town, I told her. The place is bumper-to-bumper tourists all summer, I said. But she acted as if she never got my letters, and came anyway. Then, after she'd been in town a little less than a month, she told me she hated the place. She acted as if it were my fault she'd moved here and my fault she found everything so disagreeable. She started calling me up and telling me how crummy the place was. "Laying guilt trips," Jill called it. She told me the bus service was terrible and the drivers unfriendly. As for the people at the Senior Citizens – well, she didn't want to play casino. "They can go to hell," she said, "and take their card games with them." The clerks at the supermarket were surly, the guys in the service station didn't give a damn about her or her car. And she'd made up her mind about the man she rented from, Larry Hadlock. King Larry, she called him. "He thinks he's *superior* to everyone because he has some shacks for rent and a few dollars. I wish to God I'd never laid eyes on him."

It was too hot for her when she arrived, in August, and in September it started to rain. It rained almost every day for weeks. In October it turned cold. There was snow in November and December. But long before that she began to put the bad mouth on the place and the people to the extent that I didn't want to hear about it any more, and I told her so finally. She cried, and I hugged her and thought that was the end of it. But a few days later she started in again, same stuff. Just before Christmas she called to see when I was coming by with her presents. She hadn't put up a tree and didn't intend to, she said. Then she said something else. She said if this weather didn't improve she was going to kill herself.

"Don't talk crazy," I said.

She said, "I mean it, honey. I don't want to see this place again except from my coffin. I hate this g.d. place. I don't know why I moved here. I wish I could just die and get it over with."

I remember hanging on to the phone and watching a man high up on a pole doing something to a power line. Snow whirled around his head. As I watched, he leaned out from the pole, supported only by his safety belt. Suppose he falls, I thought. I didn't have any idea what I was going to say next. I had to say something. But I was filled with unworthy feelings, thoughts no son should admit to. "You're my mother," I said finally. "What can I do to help?"

"Honey, you can't do anything," she said. "The time for doing anything has come and gone. It's too late to do anything. I wanted to like it here. I thought we'd go on picnics and take drives together. But none of that happened. You're always busy. You're off working, you and Jill. You're never at home. Or else if you are at home you have the phone off the hook all day. Anyway, I never see you," she said.

"That's not true," I said. And it wasn't. But she went on as if she hadn't heard me. Maybe she hadn't.

"Besides," she said, "this weather's killing me. It's too damned cold here. Why didn't you tell me this was the North Pole? If you had, I'd never have come. I want to go back to California, honey. I can get out and go places there. I don't know anywhere to go here. There are people back in California. I've got friends there who care what happens to me. Nobody gives a damn here. Well, I just pray I can get through to June. If I can make it that long, if I can last to June, I'm leaving this place for ever. This is the worst place I've ever lived in."

What could I say? I didn't know what to say. I couldn't even say anything about the weather. Weather was a real sore point. We said goodbye and hung up.

Other people take vacations in the summer, but my mother moves. She started moving years ago, after my dad lost his job. When that happened, when he was laid off, they sold their home, as if this were what they should do, and went to where they thought things would be better. But things weren't any better there, either. They moved again. They kept on moving. They lived in rented houses, apartments, mobile homes, and motel units even. They kept moving, lightening their load with each move they made. A couple of times they landed in a town where I lived. They'd move in with my wife and me for a while and then they'd move on again. They were like migrating animals in this regard, except there was no pattern to their movement. They moved around for years, sometimes even leaving the state for what they thought would be greener pastures. But mostly they stayed in Northern California and did their moving there. Then my dad died, and I thought my mother would stop moving and stay in one place for a while. But she didn't. She kept moving. I suggested once that she go to a psychiatrist. I even said I'd pay for it. But she wouldn't hear of it. She packed and moved out of town instead. I was desperate about things or I wouldn't have said that about the psychiatrist.

She was always in the process of packing or else unpacking. Sometimes she'd move two or three times in the same year. She talked bitterly about the place she was leaving and optimistically about the place she was going to. Her mail got fouled up, her benefit cheques went off somewhere else, and she spent hours writing letters, trying to get it all straightened out. Sometimes she'd move out of an apartment house, move to another one a few blocks away, and then, a month later, move back to the place she'd left, only to a different floor or a different side of the building. That's why when she moved here I rented a house for her and saw to it that it was furnished to her liking. "Moving around keeps her alive," Jill said. "It gives her something to do. She must get some kind of weird enjoyment out of it, I guess." But enjoyment or not, Jill thinks my mother must be losing her mind. I think so, too. But how do you tell your mother this? How do you deal with her if this is the case? Crazy doesn't stop her from planning and getting on with her next move.

She is waiting at the back door for us when we pull in. She's seventy years old, has grey hair, wears glasses with rhinestone frames, and has never been sick a day in her life. She hugs Jill, and then she hugs me. Her eyes are bright, as if she's been drinking. But she doesn't drink. She quit years ago, after my dad went on the wagon. We finish hugging and go inside. It's around five in the afternoon. I smell whatever it is drifting out of her kitchen and remember I haven't eaten since breakfast. My buzz has worn off.

"I'm starved," I say.

"Something smells good," Jill says.

"I hope it tastes good," my mother says. "I hope this chicken's done." She raises the lid on a fry pan and pushes a fork into a chicken breast. "If there's anything I can't stand, it's raw chicken. I think it's done. Why don't you sit down? Sit anyplace. I still can't regulate my stove. The burners heat up too fast. I don't like electric stoves and never have. Move that junk off the chair, Jill. I'm living here like a damned gypsy. But not for much longer, I hope." She sees me looking around for the ashtray. "Behind you," she says. "On the windowsill, honey. Before you sit down, why don't you pour us some of that Pepsi? You'll have to use these paper cups. I should have told you to bring some glasses. Is the Pepsi cold? I don't have any ice. This icebox won't keep anything cold. It isn't worth a damn. My ice cream turns to soup. It's the worst icebox I've ever had."

She forks the chicken on to a plate and puts the plate on the table along with beans and coleslaw and white bread. Then she looks to see if there is anything she's forgetting. Salt and pepper! "Sit down," she says.

We draw our chairs up to the table, and Jill takes the plates out of the sack and hands them around the table to us. "Where are you going to live when you go back?" she says. "Do you have a place lined up?"

My mother passes the chicken to Jill and says, "I wrote that lady I rented from before. She wrote back and said she had a nice first-floor place I could have. It's close to the bus stop and there's lots of stores in the area. There's a bank and a Safeway. It's the nicest place. I don't know why I left there." She says that and helps herself to some coleslaw.

"Why'd you leave then?" Jill says. "If it was so nice and all." She picks up her drumstick, looks at it, and takes a bite of the meat.

"I'll tell you why. There was an old alcoholic woman who lived next door to me. She drank from morning to night. The walls were so thin I could hear her munching ice cubes all day. She had to use a walker to get around, but that still didn't stop her. I'd hear that walker *scrape, scrape* against the floor from morning to night. That and her icebox door closing." She shakes her head at all she had to put up with. "I had to get out of there. *Scrape, scrape* all day. I couldn't stand it. I just couldn't live like that. This time I told the manager I didn't want to be next to any alcoholics. And I didn't want anything on the second floor. The second floor looks out on the parking lot. Nothing to see from there." She waits for Jill to say something more. But Jill doesn't comment. My mother looks over at me.

I'm eating like a wolf and don't say anything, either. In any case, there's nothing more to say on the subject. I keep chewing and look over at the boxes stacked against the fridge. Then I help myself to more coleslaw.

Pretty soon I finish and push my chair back. Larry Hadlock pulls up in back of the house, next to my car, and takes a lawn mower out of his pick-up. I watch him through the window behind the table. He doesn't look in our direction.

"What's he want?" my mother says and stops eating.

"He's going to cut your grass, it looks like," I say.

"It doesn't need cutting," she says. "He cut it last week. What's there for him to cut?"

"It's for the new tenant," Jill says. "Whoever that turns out to be."

My mother takes this in and then goes back to eating.

Larry Hadlock starts his mower and begins to cut the grass. I know him a little. He lowered the rent twenty-five a month when I told him it was my mother. He is a widower – a big fellow, mid-sixties. An unhappy man with a good sense of humour. His arms are covered with white hair, and white hair stands out from under his cap. He looks like a magazine illustration of a farmer. But he isn't a farmer. He is a retired construction worker who's saved a little money. For a while, in the beginning, I let myself imagine that he and my mother might take some meals together and become friends.

"There's the king," my mother says. "King Larry. Not everyone has as much money as he does and can live in a big house and charge other people high rents. Well, I hope I never see his cheap old face again once I leave here. Eat the rest of this chicken," she says to me. But I shake my head and light a cigarette. Larry pushes his mower past the window.

"You won't have to look at it much longer," Jill says.

"I'm sure glad of that, Jill. But I know he won't give me my deposit back."

"How do you know that?" I say.

"I just know," she says. "I've had dealings with his kind before. They're out for all they can get."

Jill says, "It won't be long now and you won't have to have anything more to do with him."

"I'll be so glad."

"But it'll be somebody just like him," Jill says.

19

"I don't want to think that, Jill," my mother says.

She makes coffee while Jill clears the table. I rinse the cups. Then I pour coffee, and we step around a box marked "Knickknacks" and take our cups into the living room.

Larry Hadlock is at the side of the house. Traffic moves slowly on the street out in front, and the sun has started down over the trees. I can hear the commotion the mower makes. Some crows leave the phone line and settle on to the newly cut grass in the front yard.

"I'm going to miss you, honey," my mother says. Then she says, "I'll miss you, too, Jill. I'm going to miss both of you."

Jill sips from her coffee and nods. Then she says, "I hope you have a safe trip back and find the place you're looking for at the end of the road."

"When I get settled – and this is my last move, so help me – I hope you'll come and visit," my mother says. She looks at me and waits to be reassured.

"We will," I say. But even as I say it I know it isn't true. My life caved in on me down there, and I won't be going back.

"I wish you could have been happier here," Jill says. "I wish you'd been able to stick it out or something. You know what? Your son is worried sick about you."

"Jill," I say.

But she gives her head a little shake and goes on. "Sometimes he can't sleep over it. He wakes up sometimes in the night and says, 'I can't sleep. I'm thinking about my mother.' There," she says and looks at me. "I've said it. But it was on my mind."

"How do you think I must feel?" my mother says. Then she says, "Other women my age can be happy. Why can't I be like other women? All I want is a house and a town to live in that will make me happy. That isn't a crime, is it? I hope not. I hope I'm not asking too much out of life." She puts

20

her cup on the floor next to her chair and waits for Jill to tell her she isn't asking for too much. But Jill doesn't say anything, and in a minute my mother begins to outline her plans to be happy.

After a time Jill lowers her eyes to her cup and has some more coffee. I can tell she's stopped listening. But my mother keeps talking anyway. The crows work their way through the grass in the front yard. I hear the mower howl and then thud as it picks up a clump of grass in the blade and comes to a stop. In a minute, after several tries, Larry gets it going again. The crows fly off, back to their wire. Jill picks at a fingernail. My mother is saying that the secondhand-furniture dealer is coming around the next morning to collect the things she isn't going to send on the bus or carry with her in the car. The table and chairs, TV, sofa, and bed are going with the dealer. But he's told her he doesn't have any use for the card table, so my mother is going to throw it out unless we want it.

"We'll take it," I say. Jill looks over. She starts to say something but changes her mind.

I will drive the boxes to the Greyhound station the next afternoon and start them on the way to California. My mother will spend the last night with us, as arranged. And then, early the next morning, two days from now, she'll be on her way.

She continues to talk. She talks on and on as she describes the trip she is about to make. She'll drive until four o'clock in the afternoon and then take a motel room for the night. She figures to make Eugene by dark. Eugene is a nice town – she stayed there once before, on the way up here. When she leaves the motel, she'll leave at sunrise and should, if God is looking out for her, be in California that afternoon. And God *is* looking out for her, she knows he is. How else explain her being kept around on the face of the earth? He has a plan for her. She's been praying a lot lately. She's been praying for me, too.

"Why are you praying for him?" Jill wants to know.

"Because I feel like it. Because he's my son," my mother says. "Is there anything the matter with that? Don't we all need praying for sometimes? Maybe some people don't. I don't know. What do I know any more?" She brings a hand to her forehead and rearranges some hair that's come loose from a pin.

The mower sputters off, and pretty soon we see Larry go around the house pulling the hose. He sets the hose out and then goes slowly back around the house to turn the water on. The sprinkler begins to turn.

My mother starts listing the ways she imagines Larry has wronged her since she's been in the house. But now I'm not listening, either. I am thinking how she is about to go down the highway again, and nobody can reason with her or do anything to stop her. What can I do? I can't tie her up, or commit her, though it may come to that eventually. I worry for her, and she is a heartache to me. She is all the family I have left. I'm sorry she didn't like it here and wants to leave. But I'm never going back to California. And when that's clear to me I understand something else, too. I understand that after she leaves I'm probably never going to see her again.

I look over at my mother. She stops talking. Jill raises her eyes. Both of them look at me.

"What is it, honey?" my mother says.

"What's wrong?" Jill says.

I lean forward in the chair and cover my face with my hands. I sit like that for a minute, feeling bad and stupid for doing it. But I can't help it. And the woman who brought me into this life, and this other woman I picked up with less than a year ago, they exclaim together and rise and come over to where I sit with my head in my hands like a fool. I don't open my eyes. I listen to the sprinkler whipping the grass.

"What's wrong? What's the matter?" they say.

"It's OK," I say. And in a minute it is. I open my eyes and bring my head up. I reach for a cigarette.

"See what I mean?" Jill says. "You're driving him crazy. He's going crazy with worry over you." She is on one side of my chair, and my mother is on the other side. They could tear me apart in no time at all.

"I wish I could die and get out of everyone's way," my mother says quietly. "So help me Hannah, I can't take much more of this."

"How about some more coffee?" I say. "Maybe we ought to catch the news," I say. "Then I guess Jill and I better head for home."

Two days later, early in the morning, I say goodbye to my mother for what may be the last time. I've let Jill sleep. It won't hurt if she's late to work for a change. The dogs can wait for their baths and trimmings and such. My mother holds my arm as I walk her down the steps to the driveway and open the car door for her. She is wearing white slacks and a white blouse and white sandals. Her hair is pulled back and tied with a scarf. That's white, too. It's going to be a nice day, and the sky is clear and already blue.

On the front seat of the car I see maps and a thermos of coffee. My mother looks at these things as if she can't recall having come outside with them just a few minutes ago. She turns to me then and says, "Let me hug you once more. Let me love your neck. I know I won't see you for a long time." She puts an arm around my neck, draws me to her, and then begins to cry. But she stops almost at once and steps back, pushing the heel of her hand against her eyes. "I said I wouldn't do that, and I won't. But let me get a last look at you anyway. I'll miss you, honey," she says. "I'm just going to have to live through this. I've already lived through things

23

I didn't think were possible. But I'll live through this, too, I guess." She gets into the car, starts it, and runs the engine for a minute. She rolls her window down.

"I'm going to miss you," I say. And I *am* going to miss her. She's my mother, after all, and why shouldn't I miss her? But, God forgive me, I'm glad, too, that it's finally time and that she is leaving.

"Goodbye," she says. "Tell Jill thanks for supper last night. Tell her I said goodbye."

"I will," I say. I stand there wanting to say something else. But I don't know what. We keep looking at each other, trying to smile and reassure each other. Then something comes into her eyes, and I believe she is thinking about the highway and how far she is going to have to drive that day. She takes her eyes off me and looks down the road. Then she rolls her window up, puts the car into gear, and drives to the intersection, where she has to wait for the light to change. When I see she's made it into traffic and headed towards the highway, I go back in the house and drink some coffee. I feel sad for a while, and then the sadness goes away and I start thinking about other things.

A few nights later my mother calls to say she is in her new place. She is busy fixing it up, the way she does when she has a new place. She tells me I'll be happy to know she likes it just fine to be back in sunny California. But she says there's something in the air where she is living, maybe it's pollen, that is causing her to sneeze a lot. And the traffic is heavier than she remembers from before. She doesn't recall there being so much traffic in her neighbourhood. Naturally, everyone still drives like crazy down there. "California drivers," she says. "What else can you expect?" She says it's hot for this time of the year. She doesn't think the air-conditioning unit in her apartment is working right. I tell her she should talk to the manager. "She's never around when you need her," my mother says. She hopes she hasn't made a mistake in moving back to California. She waits before she says anything else.

I'm standing at the window with the phone pressed to my ear, looking out at the lights from town and at the lighted houses closer by. Jill is at the table with the catalogue, listening.

"Are you still there?" my mother asks. "I wish you'd say something."

I don't know why, but it's then I recall the affectionate name my dad used sometimes when he was talking nice to my mother – those times, that is, when he wasn't drunk. It was a long time ago, and I was a kid, but always, hearing it, I felt better, less afraid, more hopeful about the future. *"Dear,"* he'd say. He called her "dear" sometimes – a sweet name. "Dear," he'd say, "if you're going to the store, will you bring me some cigarettes?" Or "Dear, is your cold any better?" "Dear, where is my coffee cup?"

The word issues from my lips before I can think what else I want to say to go along with it. "Dear." I say it again. I call her "dear." "Dear, try not to be afraid," I say. I tell my mother I love her and I'll write to her, yes. Then I say goodbye, and I hang up.

For a while I don't move from the window. I keep standing there, looking out at the lighted houses in our neighbourhood. As I watch, a car turns off the road and pulls into a driveway. The porch light goes on. The door to the house opens and someone comes out on the porch and stands there waiting.

Jill turns the pages of her catalogue, and then she stops turning them. "This is what we want," she says. "This is more like what I had in mind. Look at this, will you." But I don't look. I don't care five cents for curtains. "What is it you see out there, honey?" Jill says. "Tell me."

What's there to tell? The people over there embrace for a minute, and then they go inside the house together. They leave the light burning. Then they remember, and it goes out.

Whoever Was Using This Bed

The call comes in the middle of the night, three in the morning, and it nearly scares us to death.

"Answer it, answer it!" my wife cries. "My God, who is it? Answer it!"

I can't find the light, but I get to the other room, where the phone is, and pick it up after the fourth ring.

"Is Bud there?" this woman says, very drunk.

"Jesus, you have the wrong number," I say, and hang up.

I turn the light on, and go into the bathroom, and that's when I hear the phone start again.

"Answer that!" my wife screams from the bedroom. "What in God's name do they want, Jack? I can't take any more."

I hurry out of the bathroom and pick up the phone.

"Bud?" the woman says. "What are you doing, Bud?"

I say, "Look here. You have a wrong number. Don't ever call this number again."

"I have to talk to Bud," she says.

I hang up, wait until it rings again, and then I take the receiver and lay it on the table beside the phone. But I hear the woman's voice say, "Bud, talk to me, please." I leave the receiver on its side on the table, turn off the light, and close the door to the room.

In the bedroom I find the lamp on and my wife, Iris, sitting against the headboard with her knees drawn up under the covers. She has a pillow behind her back, and she's more on my side than her own side. The covers are up around her shoulders. The blankets and the sheet have been pulled out from the front of the bed. If we want to go back to sleep – I want to go back to sleep, anyway – we may have to start from scratch and do this bed over again.

"What the hell was that all about?" Iris says. "We should have unplugged the phone. I guess we forgot. Try forgetting one night to unplug the phone and see what happens. I don't believe it."

After Iris and I started living together, my former wife, or else one of my kids, used to call up when we were asleep and want to harangue us. They kept doing it even after Iris and I were married. So we started unplugging our phone before we went to bed. We unplugged the phone every night of the year, just about. It was a habit. This time I slipped up, that's all.

"Some woman wanting *Bud*," I say. I'm standing there in my pyjamas, wanting to get into bed, but I can't. "She was drunk. Move over, honey. I took the phone off the hook."

"She can't call again?"

"No," I say. "Why don't you move over a little and give me some of those covers?"

She takes her pillow and puts it on the far side of the bed, against the headboard, scoots over, and then she leans back once more. She doesn't look sleepy. She looks fully awake. I get into bed and take some covers. But the covers don't feel right. I don't have any sheet; all I have is blanket. I look down and see my feet sticking out. I turn on to my side, facing her, and bring my legs up so that my feet are under the blanket. We should make up the bed again. I ought to suggest that. But I'm thinking, too, that if we kill the light now, this minute, we might be able to go right back to sleep.

"How about you turning off your light, honey?" I say, as nice as I can.

28

"Let's have a cigarette first," she says. "Then we'll go to sleep. Get us the cigarettes and the ashtray, why don't you? We'll have a cigarette."

"Let's go to sleep," I say. "Look at what time it is." The clock radio is right there beside the bed. Anyone can see it says three-thirty.

"Come on," Iris says. "I need a cigarette after all that."

I get out of bed for the cigarettes and ashtray. I have to go into the room where the phone is, but I don't touch the phone. I don't even want to look at the phone, but I do, of course. The receiver is still on its side on the table.

I crawl back in bed and put the ashtray on the quilt between us. I light a cigarette, give it to her, and then light one for myself.

She tries to remember the dream she was having when the phone rang. "I can just remember it, but I can't remember exactly. Something about, about – no I don't know what it was about now. I can't be sure. I can't remember it," she says finally. "God damn that woman and her phone call. *'Bud'*," she says. "I'd like to punch her." She puts out her cigarette and immediately lights another, blows smoke, and lets her eyes take in the chest of drawers and the window curtains. Her hair is undone and around her shoulders. She uses the ashtray and then stares over the foot of the bed, trying to remember.

But, really, I don't care what she's dreamed. I want to go back to sleep is all. I finish my cigarette and put it out and wait for her to finish. I lie still and don't say anything.

Iris is like my former wife in that when she sleeps she sometimes has violent dreams. She thrashes around in bed during the night and wakes in the morning drenched with sweat, the nightgown sticking to her body. And, like my former wife, she wants to tell me her dreams in great detail and speculate as to what this stands for or that portends. My former wife used to kick the covers off in the night and cry out in her sleep, as if someone were laying hands on her. Once, in a particularly violent dream, she hit me on the ear with her fist. I was in a dreamless sleep, but I struck out in the dark and hit her on the forehead. Then we began yelling. We both yelled and yelled. We'd hurt each other, but we were mainly scared. We had no idea what had happened until I turned the lamp on; then we sorted it out. Afterwards, we joked about it – fistfighting in our sleep. But when so much else began to happen that was far more serious we tended to forget about that night. We never mentioned it again, even when we teased each other.

Once I woke up in the night to hear Iris grinding her teeth in her sleep. It was such a peculiar thing to have going on right next to my ear that it woke me up. I gave her a little shake, and she stopped. The next morning she told me she'd had a very bad dream, but that's all she'd tell me about it. I didn't press her for details. I guess I really didn't want to know what could have been so bad that she didn't want to say. When I told her she'd been grinding her teeth in her sleep, she frowned and said she was going to have to do something about that. The next night she brought home something called a Niteguard – something she was supposed to wear in her mouth while she slept. She had to do something, she said. She couldn't afford to keep grinding her teeth; pretty soon she wouldn't have any. So she wore this protective device in her mouth for a week or so, and then she stopped wearing it. She said it was uncomfortable and, anyway, it was not very cosmetic. Who'd want to kiss a woman wearing a thing like that in her mouth, she said. She had something there, of course.

Another time I woke up because she was stroking my face and calling me Earl. I took her hand and squeezed her fingers. "What is it?" I said. "What is it, sweetheart?" But instead of answering she simply squeezed back, sighed, and then lay still again. The next morning, when I asked her what she'd dreamed the night before, she claimed not to have had any dreams.

"So who's Earl?" I said. "Who is this Earl you were talking about in your sleep?" She blushed and said she didn't know anybody named Earl and never had.

The lamp is still on and, because I don't know what else to think about, I think about that phone being off the hook. I ought to hang it up and unplug the cord. Then we have to think about sleep.

"I'll go take care of that phone," I say. "Then let's go to sleep."

Iris uses the ashtray and says, "Make sure it's unplugged this time."

I get up again and go to the other room, open the door, and turn on the light. The receiver is still on its side on the table. I bring it to my ear, expecting to hear the dial tone. But I don't hear anything, not even the tone.

On an impulse, I say something. "Hello," I say.

"Oh, Bud, it's you," the woman says.

I hang up the phone and bend over and unplug it from the wall before it can ring again. This is a new one on me. This deal is a mystery, this woman and her Bud person. I don't know how to tell Iris about this new development, because it'll just lead to more discussion and further speculation. I decide not to say anything for now. Maybe I'll say something over breakfast.

Back in the bedroom I see she is smoking another cigarette. I see, too, that it's nearly four in the morning. I'm starting to worry. When it's four o'clock it'll soon be five o'clock, and then it will be six, then six-thirty, then time to get up for work. I lie back down, close my eyes, and decide I'll count to sixty, slowly, before I say anything else about the light.

"I'm starting to remember," Iris says. "It's coming back to me. You want to hear it, Jack?"

I stop counting, open my eyes, sit up. The bedroom is filled with smoke. I light one up, too. Why not? The hell with it.

She says, "There was a party going on in my dream."

"Where was I when this was going on?" Usually, for whatever reason, I don't figure in her dreams. It irritates me a little, but I don't let on. My feet are uncovered again. I pull them under the covers, raise myself up on my elbow, and use the ashtray. "Is this another dream that I'm not in? It's OK, if that's the case." I pull on the cigarette, hold the smoke, let it out.

"Honey, you weren't in the dream," Iris says. "I'm sorry, but you weren't. You weren't anywhere around. I *missed* you, though. I did miss you, I'm sure of it. It was like I knew you were somewhere nearby, but you weren't there where I needed you. You know how I get into those anxiety states sometimes? If we go someplace together where there's a group of people and we get separated and I can't find you? It was a little like that. You were there, I think, but I couldn't find you."

"Go ahead and tell me about the dream," I say.

She rearranges the covers around her waist and legs and reaches for a cigarette. I hold the lighter for her. Then she goes on to describe this party where all that was being served was beer. "I don't even like beer," she says. But she drank a large quantity anyway, and just when she went to leave – to go home, she says – this little dog took hold of the hem of her dress and made her stay.

She laughs, and I laugh right along with her, even though, when I look at the clock, I see the hands are close to saying four-thirty.

There was some kind of music being played in her dream – a piano, maybe, or else it was an accordion, who knows? Dreams are that way sometimes, she says. Anyway, she vaguely remembers her former husband putting in an appearance. He might have been the one serving the beer. People were drinking beer from a keg, using plastic cups. She thought she might even have danced with him.

"Why are you telling me this?"

She says, "It was a dream, honey."

"I don't think I like it, knowing you're supposed to be here beside me all night but instead you're dreaming about strange dogs, parties, and ex-husbands. I don't like you dancing with him. What the hell is this? What if I told you I dreamed I danced the night away with Carol? Would you like it?"

"It's just a dream, right?" she says. "Don't get weird on me. I won't say any more. I see I can't. I can see it isn't a good idea." She brings her fingers to her lips slowly, the way she does sometimes when she's thinking. Her face shows how hard she's concentrating; little lines appear on her forehead. "I'm sorry that you weren't in the dream. But if I told you otherwise I'd be lying to you, right?"

I nod. I touch her arm to show her it's OK. I don't really mind. And I don't, I guess. "What happened then, honey? Finish telling the dream," I say. "And maybe we can go to sleep then." I guess I wanted to know the next thing. The last I'd heard, she'd been dancing with Jerry. If there was more, I needed to hear it.

She plumps up the pillow behind her back and says, "That's all I can remember. I can't remember any more about it. That was when the goddamn phone rang."

"Bud," I say. I can see smoke drifting in the light under the lamp, and smoke hangs in the air in the room. "Maybe we should open a window," I say.

"That's a good idea," she says. "Let some of this smoke out. It can't be any good for us."

"Hell, no, it isn't," I say.

I get up again and go to the window and raise it a few inches. I can feel the cool air that comes in and from a distance

I hear a truck gearing down as it starts up the grade that will take it to the pass and on over into the next state.

"I guess pretty soon we're going to be the last smokers left in America," she says. "Seriously, we should think about quitting." She says this as she puts her cigarette out and reaches for the pack next to the ashtray.

"It's open season on smokers," I say.

I get back in the bed. The covers are turned every which way, and it's five o'clock in the morning. I don't think we're going to sleep any more tonight. But so what if we don't? Is there a law on the books? Is something bad going to happen to us if we don't?

She takes some of her hair between her fingers. Then she pushes it behind her ear, looks at me, and says, "Lately I've been feeling this vein in my forehead. It *pulses* sometimes. It throbs. Do you know what I'm talking about? I don't know if you've ever had anything like that. I hate to think about it, but probably one of these days, I'll have a stroke or something. Isn't that how they happen? A vein in your head bursts? That's probably what'll happen to me, eventually. My mother, my grandmother, and one of my aunts died of stroke. There's a history of stroke in my family. It can run in the family, you know. It's hereditary, just like heart disease, or being too fat, or whatever. Anyway," she says, "something's going to happen to me someday, right? So maybe that's what it'll be – a stroke. Maybe that's how I'll go. That's what it feels like it could be the beginning of. First it pulses a little, like it wants my attention, and then it starts to throb. Throb, throb, throb. It scares me silly," she says. "I want us to give up these goddamn cigarettes before it's too late." She looks at what's left of her cigarette, mashes it into the ashtray, and tries to fan the smoke away.

I'm on my back, studying the ceiling, thinking that this is the kind of talk that could only take place at five in the morning. I feel I ought to say something. "I get winded easy,"

I say. "I found myself out of breath when I ran in there to answer the phone."

"That could have been because of anxiety," Iris says. "Who needs it, anyway! The *idea* of somebody calling at this hour! I could tear that woman limb from limb."

I pull myself up in the bed and lean back against the headboard. I put the pillow behind my back and try to get comfortable, same as Iris. "I'll tell you something I haven't told you," I say. "Once in a while my heart palpitates. It's like it goes crazy." She's watching me closely, listening for whatever it is I'm going to say next. "Sometimes it feels like it's going to jump out of my chest. I don't know what the hell causes it."

"Why didn't you tell me?" she says. She takes my hand and holds it. She squeezes my hand. "You never said anything, honey. Listen, I don't know what I'd *do* if something ever happened to you. I'd fold up. How often does it happen? That's scary, you know." She's still holding my hand. But her fingers slide to my wrist, where my pulse is. She goes on holding my wrist like this.

"I never told you because I didn't want to scare you," I say. "But it happens sometimes. It happened as recently as a week ago. I don't have to be doing anything in particular when it happens, either. I can be sitting in a chair with the paper. Or else driving the car, or pushing a grocery basket. It doesn't matter if I'm exerting myself or not. It just starts – boom, boom, boom. Like that. I'm surprised people can't hear it. It's that loud, I think. *I* can hear it, anyway, and I don't mind telling you it scares me," I say. "So if emphysema doesn't get me, or lung cancer, or maybe a stroke like what you're talking about, then it's going to be a heart attack probably."

I reach for the cigarettes. I give her one. We're through with sleep for the night. Did we sleep? For a minute, I can't remember.

"Who knows what we'll die of?" Iris says. "It could be anything. If we live long enough, maybe it'll be kidney failure, or something like that. A friend of mine at work, her father just died of kidney failure. That's what can happen to you sometimes if you're lucky enough to get really old. When your kidneys fail, the body starts filling up with uric acid then. You finally turn a whole different colour before you die."

"Great. That sounds wonderful," I say. "Maybe we should get off this subject. How'd we get on to this stuff, anyway?"

She doesn't answer. She leans forward, away from her pillow, arms clasping her legs. She closes her eyes and lays her head on her knees. Then she begins to rock back and forth, slowly. It's as if she were listening to music. But there isn't any music. None that I can hear, anyway.

"You know what I'd like?" she says. She stops moving, opens her eyes, and tilts her head at me. Then she grins, so I'll know she's all right.

"What would you like, honey?" I've got my leg hooked over her leg, at the ankle.

She says, "I'd like some coffee, that's what. I could go for a nice strong cup of black coffee. We're awake, aren't we? Who's going back to sleep? Let's have some coffee."

"We drink too much coffee," I say. "All that coffee isn't good for us, either. I'm not saying we shouldn't have any, I'm just saying we drink too much of it. It's just an observation," I add. "Actually, I could drink some coffee myself."

"Good," she says.

But neither of us makes a move.

She shakes out her hair and then lights another cigarette. Smoke drifts slowly in the room. Some of it drifts towards the open window. A little rain begins to fall on the patio outside the window. The alarm comes on, and I reach over and shut it off. Then I take the pillow and put it under my head again. I lie back and stare at the ceiling some more. "What happened to that bright idea we had about a girl who could bring us our coffee in bed?" I say.

"I wish *somebody* would bring us coffee," she says. "A girl or a boy, one or the other. I could really go for some coffee right now."

She moves the ashtray to the nightstand, and I think she's going to get up. Somebody has to get up and start the coffee and put a can of frozen juice in the blender. One of us has to make a move. But what she does instead is slide down in the bed until she's sitting somewhere in the middle. The covers are all over the place. She picks at something on the quilt, and then rubs her palm across whatever it is before she looks up. "Did you see in the paper where that guy took a shotgun into an intensive-care unit and made the nurses take his father off the life-support machine? Did you read about that?" Iris says.

"I saw something about it on the news," I say. "But mostly they were talking about this nurse who unplugged six or eight people from their machines. At this point they don't know exactly how many she unplugged. She started off by unplugging her mother, and then she went on from there. It was like a spree, I guess. She said she thought she was doing everybody a favour. She said she hoped somebody'd do it for *her*, if they cared about her."

Iris decides to move on down to the foot of the bed. She positions herself so that she is facing me. Her legs are still under the covers. She puts her legs between my legs and says, "What about that quadriplegic woman on the news who says she wants to die, wants to starve herself to death? Now she's suing her doctor and the hospital because they insist on force-feeding her to keep her alive. Can you believe it? It's insane. They strap her down three times a day so they can run this tube into her throat. They feed her breakfast, lunch, and dinner that way. And they keep her plugged into this machine, too, because her lungs don't want to work on their own. It said in the paper that she's *begging* them to unplug her, or else to just let her starve to death. She's having to plead with them to let her die, but they won't listen. She said she started out wanting to die with some dignity. Now she's just mad and looking to sue everybody. Isn't that amazing? Isn't that one for the books?" she says. "I have these headaches sometimes," she says. "Maybe it has something to do with the vein. Maybe not. Maybe they're not related. But I don't tell you when my head hurts, because I don't want to worry you."

"What are you talking about?" I say. "Look at me. Iris? I have a right to know. I'm your husband, in case you've forgotten. If something's wrong with you, I should know about it."

"But what could you *do*? You'd just worry." She bumps my leg with her leg, then bumps it again. "Right? You'd tell me to take some aspirin. I know you."

I look towards the window, where it's beginning to get light. I can feel a damp breeze from the window. It's stopped raining now, but it's one of those mornings where it could begin to pour. I look at her again. "To tell you the truth, Iris, I get sharp pains in my side from time to time." But the moment I say the words I'm sorry. She'll be concerned, and want to talk about it. We ought to be thinking of showers; we should be sitting down to breakfast.

"Which side?" she says.

"Right side."

"It could be your appendix," she says. "Something fairly simple like that."

I shrug. "Who knows? I don't know. All I know is it happens. Every so often, for just a minute or two, I feel something sharp down there. Very sharp. At first I thought

38

it might be a pulled muscle. Which side's your gall bladder on, by the way? Is it the left or right side? Maybe it's my gall bladder. Or else maybe a gall*stone*, whatever the hell that is."

"It's not really a stone," she says. "A gallstone is like a little granule, or something like that. It's about as big as the tip of a pencil. No, wait, that might be a *kidney* stone I'm talking about. I guess I don't know anything about it." She shakes her head.

"What's the difference between kidney stone and gall-stone?" I say. "Christ, we don't even know which side of the body they're on. You don't know, and I don't know. That's how much we know together. A total of nothing. But I read somewhere that you can pass a kidney stone, if that's what this is, and usually it won't kill you. Painful, yes. I don't know what they say about a gallstone."

"I like that 'usually'," she says.

"I know," I say. "Listen, we'd better get up. It's getting really late. It's seven o'clock."

"I know," she says. "OK." But she continues to sit there. Then she says, "My grandma had arthritis so bad towards the end she couldn't get around by herself, or even move her fingers. She had to sit in a chair and wear these mittens all day. Finally, she couldn't even hold a cup of cocoa. That's how bad her arthritis was. Then she had her stroke. And my *grandpa*," she says. "He went into a nursing home not long after grandma died. It was either that or else somebody had to come in and be with him around the clock, and nobody could do that. Nobody had the money for twenty-four-hour-a-day care, either. So he goes into the nursing home. But he began to deteriorate fast in there. One time, after he'd been in that place for a while, my mom went to visit him and then she came home and said something. I'll never forget what she said." She looks at me as if I'm never going to forget it, either. And I'm not. "She said, 'My dad doesn't recognize me any more. He doesn't even know who I am. My dad has become a vegetable.' That was my mom who said that."

She leans over and covers her face with her hands and begins to cry. I move down there to the foot of the bed and sit beside her. I take her hand and hold it in my lap. I put my arm around her. We're sitting together looking at the headboard and at the nightstand. The clock's there, too, and beside the clock a few magazines and a paperback. We're sitting on the part of the bed where we keep our feet when we sleep. It looks like whoever was using this bed left in a hurry. I know I won't ever look at this bed again without remembering it like this. We're into something now, but I don't know what, exactly.

"I don't want anything like that to ever happen to me," she says. "Or to you, either." She wipes her face with a corner of the blanket and takes a deep breath, which comes out as a sob. "I'm sorry. I just can't help it," she says.

"It won't happen to us. It won't," I say. "Don't worry about any of it, OK? We're fine, Iris, and we're going to stay fine. In any case, that time's a long time off. Hey, I love you. We love each other, don't we? That's the important thing. That's what counts. Don't worry, honey."

"I want you to promise me something," she says. She takes her hand back. She moves my arm away from her shoulder. "I want you to promise me you'll pull the plug on me, if and when it's ever necessary. If it ever comes to that, I mean. Do you hear what I'm saying? I'm serious about this, Jack. I want you to pull the plug on me if you ever have to. Will you promise?"

I don't say anything right away. What am I supposed to say? They haven't written the book on this one yet. I need a minute to think. I know it won't cost me anything to tell her I'll do whatever she wants. It's just words, right? Words are easy. But there's more to it than this; she wants an honest response from me. And I don't know what I feel about it yet. I shouldn't be hasty. I can't say something without thinking about what I'm saying, about consequences, about what she's going to feel when I say it – whatever it is I say.

I'm still thinking about it when she says, "What about you?"

"What about me what?"

"Do you want to be unplugged if it comes to that? God forbid it ever does, of course," she says. "But I should have some kind of idea, you know – some word from you now – about what you want me to do if worst comes to worst." She's looking at me closely, waiting for me to say. She wants something she can file away to use later, if and when she ever has to. Sure. OK. Easy enough for me to say, *Unplug me, honey, if you think it's for the best.* But I need to consider this a little more. I haven't even said yet what I will or won't do for *her.* Now I have to think about me and *my* situation. I don't feel I should jump into this. This is nuts. *We're* nuts. But I realize that whatever I say now might come back to me sometime. It's important. This is a life-and-death thing we're talking about here.

She hasn't moved. She's still waiting for her answer. And I can see we're not going anywhere this morning until she has an answer. I think about it some more, and then I say what I mean. "No. Don't unplug me. I don't want to be unplugged. Leave me hooked up just as long as possible. Who's going to object? Are you going to object? Will I be offending anybody? As long as people can stand the sight of me, just so long as they don't start howling, don't unplug anything. Let me keep going, OK? Right to the bitter end. Invite my friends in to say goodbye. Don't do anything rash."

"Be serious," she says. "This is a very serious matter we're discussing."

"I am serious. Don't unplug me. It's as simple as that."

She nods. "OK, then. I promise you I won't." She hugs

me. She holds me tight for a minute. Then she lets go.
She looks at the clock radio and says, "Jesus, we better get
moving."

So we get out of bed and start getting dressed. In some ways
it's just like any other morning, except we do things faster.
We drink coffee and juice and we eat English muffins. We
remark on the weather, which is overcast and blustery. We
don't talk any more about plugs, or about sickness and hospi-
tals and stuff like that. I kiss her and leave her on the front
porch with her umbrella open, waiting for her ride to work.
Then I hurry to my car and get in. In a minute, after I've run
the motor, I wave and drive off.

But during the day, at work, I think about some of those
things we talked about this morning. I can't help it. For one
thing, I'm bone-tired from lack of sleep. I feel vulnerable and
prey to any random, gruesome thought. Once, when nobody
is around, I put my head on my desk and think I might catch
a few minutes' sleep. But when I close my eyes I find myself
thinking about it again. In my mind I can see a hospital bed.
That's all – just a hospital bed. The bed's in a room, I guess.
Then I see an oxygen tent over the bed, and beside the bed
some of those screens and some big monitors – the kind they
have in movies. I open my eyes and sit up in my chair and
light a cigarette. I drink some coffee while I smoke the
cigarette. Then I look at the time and get back to work.

At five o'clock, I'm so tired it's all I can do to drive home.
It's raining, and I have to be careful driving. Very careful.
There's been an accident, too. Someone has rear-ended someone else at a traffic light, but I don't think anyone has been
hurt. The cars are still out in the road, and people are standing
around in the rain, talking. Still, traffic moves slowly; the
police have set out flares.

When I see my wife, I say, "God, what a day. I'm whipped.

42

How are you doing?" We kiss each other. I take off my coat and hang it up. I take the drink Iris gives me. Then, because it's been on my mind, and because I want to clear the deck, so to speak, I say, "All right, if it's what you want to hear, I'll pull the plug for you. If that's what you want me to do, I'll do it. If it will make you happy, here and now, to hear me say so, I'll say it. I'll do it for you. I'll pull the plug, or have it pulled, if I ever think it's necessary. But what I said about my plug still stands. Now I don't want to have to think about this stuff ever again. I don't even want to have to *talk* about it again. I think we've said all there is to say on the subject. We've exhausted every angle. *I'm* exhausted."

Iris grins. "OK," she says. "At least I know now, anyway. I didn't before. Maybe I'm crazy, but I feel better somehow, if you want to know. I don't want to think about it any more, either. But I'm glad we talked it over. I'll never bring it up again, either, and that's a promise."

She takes my drink and puts it on the table, next to the phone. She puts her arms around me and holds me and lets her head rest on my shoulder. But here's the thing. What I've just said to her, what I've been thinking about off and on all day, well, I feel as if I've crossed some kind of invisible line. I feel as if I've come to a place I never thought I'd have to come to. And I don't know how I got here. It's a strange place. It's a place where a little harmless dreaming and then some sleepy, early-morning talk has led me into considerations of death and annihilation.

The phone rings. We let go of each other, and I reach to answer it. "Hello," I say.

"Hello, there," the woman says back.

It's the same woman who called this morning, but she isn't drunk now. At least, I don't think she is; she doesn't sound drunk. She is speaking quietly, reasonably, and she is asking me if I can put her in touch with Bud Roberts. She apologizes.

43

She hates to trouble me, she says, but this is an urgent matter. She's sorry for any trouble she might be giving.

While she talks, I fumble with my cigarettes. I put one in my mouth and use the lighter. Then it's my turn to talk. This is what I say to her: "Bud Roberts doesn't live here. He is not at this number, and I don't expect he ever will be. I will never, never lay eyes on this man you're talking about. Please don't ever call here again. Just don't, OK? Do you hear me? If you're not careful, I'll wring your neck for you."

"The *gall* of that woman," Iris says.

My hands are shaking. I think my voice is doing things. But while I'm trying to tell all this to the woman, while I'm trying to make myself understood, my wife moves quickly and bends over, and that's it. The line goes dead, and I can't hear anything.

Intimacy

I have some business out west anyway, so I stop off in this
little town where my former wife lives. We haven't seen each
other in four years. But from time to time, when something
of mine appeared, or was written about me in the magazines
or papers – a profile or an interview – I sent her these things.
I don't know what I had in mind except I thought she might
be interested. In any case, she never responded.

It is nine in the morning, I haven't called, and it's true I
don't know what I am going to find.

But she lets me in. She doesn't seem surprised. We don't
shake hands, much less kiss each other. She takes me into the
living room. As soon as I sit down she brings me some coffee.
Then she comes out with what's on her mind. She says I've
caused her anguish, made her feel exposed and humiliated.

Make no mistake, I feel I'm home.

She says, But then you were into betrayal early. You always
felt comfortable with betrayal. No, she says, that's not true.
Not in the beginning, at any rate. You were different then.
But I guess I was different too. Everything was different, she
says. No, it was after you turned thirty-five, or thirty-six,
whenever it was, around in there anyway, your mid-thirties
somewhere, then you started in. You really started in. You
turned on me. You did it up pretty then. You must be proud
of yourself.

She says, Sometimes I could scream.

45

She says she wishes I'd forget about the hard times, the bad times, when I talk about back then. Spend some time on the good times, she says. Weren't there some good times? She wishes I'd get off that other subject. She's bored with it. Sick of hearing about it. Your private hobbyhorse, she says. What's done is done and water under the bridge, she says. A tragedy, yes. God knows it was a tragedy and then some. But why keep it going? Don't you ever get tired of dredging up that old business?

She says, Let go of the past, for Christ's sake. Those old hurts. You must have some other arrows in your quiver, she says.

She says, You know something? I think you're sick. I think you're crazy as a bedbug. Hey, you don't believe the things they're saying about you, do you? Don't believe them for a minute, she says. Listen, I could tell them a thing or two. Let them talk to me about it, if they want to hear a story.

She says, Are you listening to me?

I'm listening, I say. I'm all ears, I say.

She says, I've really had a bellyful of it, buster! Who asked you here today anyway? I sure as hell didn't. You just show up and walk in. What the hell do you want from me? Blood? You want more blood? I thought you had your fill by now.

She says, Think of me as dead. I want to be left in peace now. That's all I want any more is to be left in peace and forgotten about. Hey, I'm forty-five years old, she says. Forty-five going on fifty-five, or sixty-five. Lay off, will you.

She says, Why don't you wipe the blackboard clean and see what you have left after that? Why don't you start with a clean slate? See how far that gets you, she says.

She has to laugh at this. I laugh too, but it's nerves.

She says, You know something? I had my chance once, but I let it go. I just let it go. I don't guess I ever told you. But now look at me. Look! Take a good look while you're at it. You threw me away, you son of a bitch.

46

She says, I was younger then and a better person. Maybe you were too, she says. A better person, I mean. You had to be. You were better then or I wouldn't have had anything to do with you.

She says, I loved you so much once. I loved you to the point of distraction. I did. More than anything in the whole wide world. Imagine that. What a laugh that is now. Can you imagine it? We were so *intimate* once upon a time I can't believe it now. I think that's the strangest thing of all now. The memory of being that intimate with somebody. We were so intimate I could puke. I can't imagine ever being that intimate with somebody else. I haven't been.

She says, Frankly, and I mean this, I want to be kept out of it from here on out. Who do you think you are anyway? You think you're God or somebody? You're not fit to lick God's boots, or anybody else's for that matter. Mister, you've been hanging out with the wrong people. But what do I know? I don't even know what I know any longer. I know I don't like what you've been dishing out. I know that much. You know what I'm talking about, don't you? Am I right?

Right, I say. Right as rain.

She says, You'll agree to anything, won't you? You give in too easy. You always did. You don't have any principles, not one. Anything to avoid a fuss. But that's neither here nor there.

She says, You remember that time I pulled the knife on you?

She says this as if in passing, as if it's not important.

Vaguely, I say. I must have deserved it, but I don't remember much about it. Go ahead, why don't you, and tell me about it.

She says, I'm beginning to understand something now. I think I know why you're here. Yes. I know why you're here, even if you don't. But you're a slyboots. You know why you're here. You're on a fishing expedition. You're hunting for *material*. Am I getting warm? Am I right?

Tell me about the knife, I say.

She says, If you want to know, I'm real sorry I didn't use that knife. I am. I really and truly am. I've thought and thought about it, and I'm sorry I didn't use it. I had the chance. But I hesitated. I hesitated and was lost, as somebody or other said. But I should have used it, the hell with everything and everybody. I should have nicked your arm with it at least. At least that.

Well, you didn't, I say. I thought you were going to cut me with it, but you didn't. I took it away from you.

She says, You were always lucky. You took it away and then you slapped me. Still, I regret I didn't use that knife just a little bit. Even a little would have been something to remember me by.

I remember a lot, I say. I say that, then wish I hadn't.

She says, Amen, brother. That's the bone of contention here, if you hadn't noticed. That's the whole problem. But like I said, in my opinion you remember the wrong things. You remember the low, shameful things. That's why you got interested when I brought up the knife.

She says, I wonder if you ever have any regret. For whatever that's worth on the market these days. Not much, I guess. But you ought to be a specialist in it by now.

Regret, I say. It doesn't interest me much, to tell the truth. Regret is not a word I use very often. I guess I mainly don't have it. I admit I hold to the dark view of things. Sometimes, anyway. But regret? I don't think so.

She says, You're a real son of a bitch, did you know that? A ruthless, cold-hearted son of a bitch. Did anybody ever tell you that?

You did, I say. Plenty of times.

She says, I always speak the truth. Even when it hurts. You'll never catch me in a lie.

She says, My eyes were opened a long time ago, but by then it was too late. I had my chance but I let it slide through my fingers. I even thought for a while you'd come back. Why'd I think that anyway? I must have been out of my mind. I could cry my eyes out now, but I wouldn't give you that satisfaction.

She says, You know what? I think if you were on fire right now, if you suddenly burst into flame this minute, I wouldn't throw a bucket of water on you.

She laughs at this. Then her face closes down again.

She says, Why in hell *are* you here? You want to hear some more? I could go on for days. I think I know why you turned up, but I want to hear it from you.

When I don't answer, when I just keep sitting there, she goes on.

She says, After that time, when you went away, nothing much mattered after that. Not the kids, not God, not anything. It was like I didn't know what hit me. It was like I had *stopped living*. My life had been going along, going along, and then it just stopped. It didn't just come to a stop, it screeched to a stop. I thought, If I'm not worth anything to him, well, I'm not worth anything to myself or anybody else either. That was the worst thing I felt. I thought my heart would break. What am I saying? It did break. Of course it broke. It broke, just like that. It's still broke, if you want to know. And so there you have it in a nutshell. My eggs in one basket, she says. A tisket, a tasket. All my rotten eggs in one basket.

She says, You found somebody else for yourself, didn't you? It didn't take long. And you're happy now. That's what they say about you anyway: "He's happy now." Hey, I read everything you send! You think I don't? Listen, I know your heart, mister. I always did. I knew it back then, and I know it now. I know your heart inside and out, and don't you ever forget it. Your heart is a jungle, a dark forest, it's a garbage pail, if you want to know. Let them talk to me if they want

49

to ask somebody something. I know how you operate. Just let them come around here, and I'll give them an earful. I was there. I served, buddy boy. Then you held me up for display and ridicule in your so-called work. For any Tom or Harry to pity or pass judgement on. Ask me if I cared. Ask me if it embarrassed me. Go ahead, ask.

No, I say, I won't ask that. I don't want to get into that, I say.

Damn straight you don't! she says. And you know *why*, too!

She says, Honey, no offence, but sometimes I think I could shoot you and watch you kick.

She says, You can't look me in the eyes, can you?

She says, and this is exactly what she says, You can't even look me in the eyes when I'm talking to you.

So, OK, I look her in the eyes.

She says, Right. OK, she says. Now we're getting someplace, maybe. That's better. You can tell a lot about the person you're talking to from his eyes. Everybody knows that. But you know something else? There's nobody in this whole world who would tell you this, but I can tell you. I have the right. I *earned* that right, sonny. You have yourself confused with somebody else. And that's the pure truth of it. But what do I know? they'll say in a hundred years. They'll say, Who was she anyway?

She says, In any case, you sure as hell have *me* confused with somebody else. Hey, I don't even have the same name any more! Not the name I was born with, not the name I lived with you with, not even the name I had two years ago. What is this? What is this in hell all about anyway? Let me say something. I want to be left alone now. Please. That's not a crime.

She says, Don't you have someplace else you should be? Some plane to catch? Shouldn't you be somewhere far from here at this very minute?

No, I say. I say it again: No. No place, I say. I don't have any place I have to be.

And then I do something. I reach over and take the sleeve of her blouse between my thumb and forefinger. That's all. I just touch it that way, and then I just bring my hand back. She doesn't draw away. She doesn't move.

Then here's the thing I do next. I get down on my knees, a big guy like me, and I take the hem of her dress. What am I doing on the floor? I wish I could say. But I know it's where I ought to be, and I'm there on my knees holding on to the hem of her dress.

She is still for a minute. But in a minute she says, Hey, it's all right, stupid. You're so dumb, sometimes. Get up now. I'm telling you to get up. Listen, it's OK. I'm over it now. It took me a while to get over it. What do you think? Did you think it wouldn't? Then you walk in here and suddenly the whole cruddy business is back. I felt a need to ventilate. But you know, and I know, it's over and done with now.

She says, For the longest while, honey, I was inconsolable. *Inconsolable*, she says. Put that word in your little notebook. I can tell you from experience that's the saddest word in the English language. Anyway, I got over it finally. Time is a gentleman, a wise man said. Or else maybe a worn-out old woman, one or the other anyway.

She says, I have a life now. It's a different kind of life than yours, but I guess we don't need to compare. It's my life, and that's the important thing I have to realize as I get older. Don't feel *too* bad, anyway, she says. I mean, it's all right to feel a *little* bad, maybe. That won't hurt you, that's only to be expected after all. Even if you can't move yourself to regret.

She says, Now you have to get up and get out of here. My husband will be along pretty soon for his lunch. How would I explain this kind of thing?

It's crazy, but I'm still on my knees holding the hem of her dress. I won't let it go. I'm like a terrier, and it's like I'm stuck to the floor. It's like I can't move.

She says, Get up now. What is it? You still want something from me. What do you want? Want me to forgive you? Is that why you're doing this? That's it, isn't it? That's the reason you came all this way. The knife thing kind of perked you up, too. I think you'd forgotten about that. But you needed me to remind you. OK, I'll say something if you'll just go.

She says, I forgive you.

She says, Are you satisfied now? Is that better? Are you happy? He's happy now, she says.

But I'm still there, knees to the floor.

She says, Did you hear what I said? You have to go now. Hey, stupid. Honey, I said I forgive you. And I even reminded you about the knife thing. I can't think what else I can do now. You got it made in the shade, baby. Come *on* now, you have to get out of here. Get up. That's right. You're still a big guy, aren't you. Here's your hat, don't forget your hat. You never used to wear a hat. I never in my life saw you in a hat before.

She says, Listen to me now. Look at me. Listen carefully to what I'm going to tell you.

She moves closer. She's about three inches from my face. We haven't been this close in a long time. I take these little breaths that she can't hear, and I wait. I think my heart slows way down, I think.

She says, You just tell it like you have to, I guess, and forget the rest. Like always. You been doing that for so long now anyway it shouldn't be hard for you.

She says, There, I've done it. You're free, aren't you? At least you think you are anyway. Free at last. That's a joke, but don't laugh. Anyway, you feel better, don't you?

She walks with me down the hall.

She says, I can't imagine how I'd explain this if my husband was to walk in this very minute. But who really cares any more, right? In the final analysis, nobody gives a damn any more. Besides which, I think everything that can happen that way has already happened. His name is Fred, by the way. He's a decent guy and works hard for his living. He cares for me.

So she walks me to the front door, which has been standing open all this while. The door that was letting in light and fresh air this morning, and sounds off the street, all of which we had ignored. I look outside and, Jesus, there's this white moon hanging in the morning sky. I can't think when I've ever seen anything so remarkable. But I'm afraid to comment on it. I am. I don't know what might happen. I might break into tears even. I might not understand a word I'd say.

She says, Maybe you'll be back sometime, and maybe you won't. This'll wear off, you know. Pretty soon you'll start feeling bad again. Maybe it'll make a good story, she says. But I don't want to know about it if it does.

I say goodbye. She doesn't say anything more. She looks at her hands, and then she puts them into the pockets of her dress. She shakes her head. She goes back inside, and this time she closes the door.

I move off down the sidewalk. Some kids are tossing a football at the end of the street. But they aren't my kids, and they aren't her kids either. There are these leaves everywhere, even in the gutters. Piles of leaves wherever I look. They're falling off the limbs as I walk. I can't take a step without putting my shoe into leaves. Somebody ought to make an effort here. Somebody ought to get a rake and take care of this.

Menudo

I can't sleep, but when I'm sure my wife Vicky is asleep, I get up and look through our bedroom window, across the street, at Oliver and Amanda's house. Oliver has been gone for three days, but his wife Amanda is awake. She can't sleep either. It's four in the morning, and there's not a sound outside – no wind, no cars, no moon even – just Oliver and Amanda's place with the lights on, leaves heaped up under the front windows.

A couple of days ago, when I couldn't sit still, I raked our yard – Vicky's and mine. I gathered all the leaves into bags, tied off the tops, and put the bags alongside the kerb. I had an urge then to cross the street and rake over there, but I didn't follow through. It's my fault things are the way they are across the street.

I've only slept a few hours since Oliver left. Vicky saw me moping around the house, looking anxious, and decided to put two and two together. She's on her side of the bed now, scrunched on to about ten inches of mattress. She got into bed and tried to position herself so she wouldn't accidentally roll into me while she slept. She hasn't moved since she lay down, sobbed, and then dropped into sleep. She's exhausted. I'm exhausted too.

I've taken nearly all of Vicky's pills, but I still can't sleep. I'm keyed up. But maybe if I keep looking I'll catch a glimpse of Amanda moving around inside her house, or else find her peering from behind a curtain, trying to see what she can see over here.

What if I do see her? So what? What then?

Vicky says I'm crazy. She said worse things too last night. But who could blame her? I told her – I had to – but I didn't tell her it was Amanda. When Amanda's name came up, I insisted it wasn't her. Vicky suspects, but I wouldn't name names. I wouldn't say who, even though she kept pressing and then hit me a few times in the head.

"What's it matter *who*?" I said. "You've never met the woman," I lied. "You don't know her." That's when she started hitting me.

I feel *wired*. That's what my painter friend Alfredo used to call it when he talked about friends of his coming down off something. *Wired*. I'm wired.

This thing is nuts. I know it is, but I can't stop thinking about Amanda. Things are so bad just now I even find myself thinking about my first wife, Molly. I loved Molly, I thought, more than my own life.

I keep picturing Amanda in her pink nightgown, the one I like on her so much, along with her pink slippers. And I feel certain she's in the big leather chair right now, under the brass reading lamp. She's smoking cigarettes, one after the other. There are two ashtrays close at hand, and they're both full. To the left of her chair, next to the lamp, there's an end table stacked with magazines – the usual magazines that nice people read. We're nice people, all of us, to a point. Right this minute, Amanda is, I imagine, paging through a magazine, stopping every so often to look at an illustration or a cartoon.

Two days ago, in the afternoon, Amanda said to me, "I can't read books any more. Who has the time?" It was the day after Oliver had left, and we were in this little café in the industrial part of the city. "Who can concentrate any more?" she said, stirring her coffee. "Who reads? Do you read?" (I shook my head.) "Somebody must read, I guess. You see all these books around in store windows, and there are those clubs. Somebody's reading," she said. "Who? I don't know anybody who reads."

That's what she said, apropos of nothing – that is, we weren't talking about books, we were talking about our *lives*. Books had nothing to do with it.

"What did Oliver say when you told him?"

Then it struck me that what we were saying – the tense, watchful expressions we wore – belonged to the people on afternoon TV programmes that I'd never done more than switch on and then off.

Amanda looked down and shook her head, as if she couldn't bear to remember.

"You didn't admit who it was you were involved with, did you?"

She shook her head again.

"You're sure of that?" I waited until she looked up from her coffee.

"I didn't mention any names, if that's what you mean."

"Did he say where he was going, or how long he'd be away?" I said, wishing I didn't have to hear myself. This was my neighbour I was talking about. Oliver Porter. A man I'd helped drive out of his home.

"He didn't say where. A hotel. He said I should make my arrangements and be gone – *be gone*, he said. It was like biblical the way he said it – out of his house, out of his *life*, in a week's time. I guess he's coming back then. So we have to decide something real important, real soon, honey. You and I have to make up our minds pretty damn quick."

It was her turn to look at me now, and I know she was looking for a sign of life-long commitment. "A week," I said. I looked at my coffee, which had gotten cold. A lot had happened in a little while, and we were trying to take it in. I don't know what long-term things, if any, we'd thought about those months as we moved from flirtation to love, and then afternoon assignations. In any case, we were in a serious fix now. Very serious. We'd never expected – not in a hundred years – to be hiding out in a café, in the middle of the afternoon, trying to decide matters like this.

I raised my eyes, and Amanda began stirring her coffee. She kept stirring it. I touched her hand, and the spoon dropped out of her fingers. She picked it up and began stirring again. We could have been anybody drinking coffee at a table under fluorescent lights in a run-down café. Anybody, just about. I took Amanda's hand and held it, and it seemed to make a difference.

Vicky's still sleeping on her side when I go downstairs. I plan to heat some milk and drink that. I used to drink whisky when I couldn't sleep, but I gave it up. Now it's strictly hot milk. In the whisky days I'd wake up with this tremendous thirst in the middle of the night. But, back then, I was always looking ahead: I kept a bottle of water in the fridge, for instance. I'd be dehydrated, sweating from head to toe when I woke, but I'd wander out to the kitchen and could count on finding that bottle of cold water in the fridge. I'd drink it, all of it, down the hatch, an entire quart of water. Once in a while I'd use a glass, but not often. Suddenly I'd be drunk all over again and weaving around the kitchen. I can't begin to account for it – sober one minute, drunk the next.

The drinking was part of my destiny – according to Molly, anyway. She put a lot of stock in destiny.

I felt wild from lack of sleep. I'd give anything, just about, to be able to go to sleep, and sleep the sleep of an honest man.

Why do we have to sleep anyway? And why do we tend to sleep less during some crises and more during others? For instance, that time my dad had his stroke. He woke up after a coma – seven days and nights in a hospital bed – and calmly said "Hello" to the people in his room. Then his eyes picked me out. "Hello, son," he said. Five minutes later, he died. Just like that – he died. But, during that whole crisis, I never took my clothes off and didn't go to bed. I may have catnapped in a waiting-room chair from time to time, but I never went to bed and *slept*.

And then a year or so ago I found out Vicky was seeing somebody else. Instead of confronting *her*, I went to bed when I heard about it, and stayed there. I didn't get up for days, a week maybe – I don't know. I mean, I got up to go to the bathroom, or else to the kitchen to make a sandwich. I even went out to the living room in my pyjamas, in the afternoon, and tried to read the papers. But I'd fall asleep sitting up. Then I'd stir, open my eyes and go back to bed and sleep some more. I couldn't get enough sleep.

It passed. We weathered it. Vicky quit her boyfriend, or he quit her, I never found out. I just know she went away from me for a while, and then she came back. But I have the feeling we're not going to weather this business. This thing is different. Oliver has given Amanda that ultimatum.

Still, isn't it possible that Oliver himself is awake at this moment and writing a letter to Amanda, urging reconciliation? Even now he might be scribbling away, trying to persuade her that what she's doing to him and their daughter Beth is foolish, disastrous, and finally a tragic thing for the three of them.

No, that's insane. I know Oliver. He's relentless, unforgiving. He could slam a croquet ball into the next block – and has. He isn't going to write any such letter. He gave her an ultimatum, right? – and that's that. A week. Four days now. Or is it three? Oliver may be awake, but if he is, he's sitting in a chair in his hotel room with a glass of iced vodka in his hand, his feet on the bed, TV turned on low. He's dressed, except for his shoes. He's not wearing shoes – that's the only concession he makes. That and the fact he's loosened his tie.

Oliver is relentless.

I heat the milk, spoon the skin from the surface and pour it up. Then I turn off the kitchen light and take the cup into the living room and sit on the sofa, where I can look across the street at the lighted windows. But I can hardly sit still. I keep fidgeting, crossing one leg and then the other. I feel like I could throw off sparks, or break a window – maybe rearrange all the furniture.

The things that go through your mind when you can't sleep! Earlier, thinking about Molly, for a moment I couldn't even remember what she *looked* like, for Christ's sake, yet we were together for years, more or less continuously, since we were kids. Molly, who said she'd love me for ever. The only thing left was the memory of her sitting and weeping at the kitchen table, her shoulders bent forward, and her hands covering her face. *For ever*, she said. But it hadn't worked out that way. Finally, she said, it didn't matter, it was of no real concern to her, if she and I lived together the rest of our lives or not. Our love existed on a "higher plane". That's what she said to Vicky over the phone that time, after Vicky and I had set up housekeeping together. Molly called, got hold of Vicky, and said, "You have your relationship with him, but I'll always have mine. His destiny and mine are linked."

My first wife, Molly, she talked like that. "Our destinies are linked." She didn't talk like that in the beginning. It was only later, after so much had happened, that she started using words like "cosmic" and "empowerment" and so forth. But our destinies are *not* linked – not now, anyway, if they ever were. I don't even know where she is now, not for certain.

I think I could put my finger on the exact time, the real

turning point, when it came undone for Molly. It was after I started seeing Vicky, and Molly found out. They called me up one day from the high school where Molly taught and said, "Please. Your wife is doing handsprings in front of the school. You'd better get down here." It was after I took her home that I began hearing about "higher power" and "going with the flow" – stuff of that sort. Our destiny had been "revised". And if I'd been hesitating before, well, I left her then as fast as I could – this woman I'd known all my life, the one who'd been my best friend for years, my intimate, my confidante. I bailed out on her. For one thing, I was scared. *Scared*.

This girl I'd started out with in life, this sweet thing, this gentle soul, she wound up going to fortune-tellers, palm readers, *crystal ball gazers*, looking for answers, trying to figure out what she should do with her life. She quit her job, drew out her teacher's retirement money, and thereafter never made a decision without consulting the *I Ching*. She began wearing strange clothes – clothes with permanent wrinkles and a lot of burgundy and orange. She even got involved wih a group that sat around, I'm not kidding, trying to levitate.

When Molly and I were growing up together, she was a part of me and, sure, I was a part of her, too. We loved each other. It *was* our destiny. I believed in it then myself. But now I don't know what to believe in. I'm not complaining, simply stating a fact. I'm down to nothing. And I have to go on like this. No destiny. Just the next thing meaning whatever you think it does. Compulsion and error, just like everybody else.

Amanda? I'd like to believe in her, bless her heart. But she was looking for somebody when she met me. That's the way with people when they get restless: they start up something, knowing that's going to change things for good.

I'd like to go out in the front yard and shout something. "None of this is worth it!" That's what I'd like people to hear.

"Destiny," Molly said. For all I know she's still talking about it.

All the lights are off over there now, except for that light in the kitchen. I could try calling Amanda on the phone. I could do that and see how far it gets me! What if Vicky heard me dialling or talking on the phone and came downstairs? What if she lifted the receiver upstairs and listened? Besides, there's always the chance Beth might pick up the phone. I don't want to talk to any kids this morning. I don't want to talk to anybody. Actually, I'd talk to Molly, if I could, but I can't any longer – she's somebody else now. She isn't *Molly* any more. But – what can I say? – I'm somebody else, too.

I wish I could be like everybody else in this neighbourhood – your basic, normal, unaccomplished person – and go up to my bedroom, and lie down, and sleep. It's going to be a big day today, and I'd like to be ready for it. I wish I could sleep and wake up and find everything in my life different. Not necessarily just the big things, like this thing with Amanda or the past with Molly. But things clearly within my power.

Take the situation with my mother: I used to send money every month. But then I started sending her the same amount in twice-yearly sums. I gave her money on her birthday, and I gave her money at Christmas. I thought: I won't have to worry about forgetting her birthday, and I won't have to worry about sending her a Christmas present. I won't have to worry, period. It went like clockwork for a long time.

Then last year she asked me – it was in between money times, it was in March, or maybe April – for a radio. A radio, she said, would make a difference to her.

What she wanted was a little clock radio. She could put it in her kitchen and have it out there to listen to while she was fixing something to eat in the evening. And she'd have the clock to look at too, so she'd know when something was supposed to come out of the oven, or how long it was until one of her programmes started.

A little clock radio.

She hinted around at first. She said, "I'd sure like to have a radio. But I can't afford one. I guess I'll have to wait for my birthday. That little radio I had, it fell and broke. I miss a radio." *I miss a radio.* That's what she said when we talked on the phone, or else she'd bring it up when she'd write.

Finally – what'd I say? I said to her over the phone that I couldn't afford any radios. I said it in a letter too, so she'd be sure and understand. *I can't afford any radios*, is what I wrote. I can't do any more, I said, than I'm doing. Those were my very words.

But it wasn't true! I could have done more. I just said I couldn't. I could have afforded to buy a radio for her. What would it have cost me? Thirty-five dollars? Forty dollars or less, including tax. I could have sent her a radio through the mail. I could have had somebody in the store do it, if I didn't want to go to the trouble myself. Or else I could have sent her a forty-dollar cheque along with a note saying, *This money is for your radio, mother.*

I could have handled it in any case. Forty dollars – are you kidding? But I didn't. I wouldn't part with it. It seemed there was a *principle* involved. That's what I told myself anyway – there's a principle involved here.

Ha.

Then what happened? She died. She *died*. She was walking home from the grocery store, back to her apartment, carrying her sack of groceries, and she fell into somebody's bushes and died.

I took a flight out there to make the arrangements. She was still at the coroner's, and they had her purse and her groceries behind the desk in the office. I didn't bother to look in the purse they handed me. But what she had from the grocery store was a jar of Metamucil, two grapefruits, a carton of cottage cheese, a quart of buttermilk, some potatoes and onions, and a package of ground meat that was beginning to change colour.

Boy! I cried when I saw those things. I couldn't stop. I didn't think I'd ever quit crying. The woman who worked at the desk was embarrassed and brought me a glass of water. They gave me a bag for my mother's groceries and another bag for her personal effects – her purse and her dentures. Later, I put the dentures in my coat pocket and drove them down in a rental car and gave them to somebody at the funeral home.

The light in Amanda's kitchen is still on. It's a bright light that spills out on to all those leaves. Maybe she's like I am, and she's scared. Maybe she left that light burning as a night-light. Or maybe she's still awake and is at the kitchen table, under the light, writing me a letter. Amanda is writing me a letter, and somehow she'll get it into my hands later on when the real day starts.

Come to think of it, I've never had a letter from her since we've known each other. All the time we've been involved – six months, eight months – and I've never once seen a scrap of her handwriting. I don't even know if she's *literate* that way.

I think she is. Sure, she is. She talks about books, doesn't she? It doesn't matter of course. Well, a little, I suppose. I love her in any case, right?

But I've never written anything to her, either. We always talked on the phone or else face to face.

Molly, she was the letter writer. She used to write me even after we weren't living together. Vicky would bring her letters in from the box and leave them on the kitchen table without a word. Finally the letters dwindled away, became more and more infrequent and bizarre. When she did write, the letters gave me a chill. They were full of talk about "auras" and "signs". Occasionally she reported a voice that was telling her something she ought to do or some place she should go. And once she told me that no matter what happened, we were still "on the same frequency". She always knew exactly what I felt, she said. She "beamed in on me", she said, from time to time. Reading those letters of hers, the hair on the back of my neck would tingle. She also had a new word for destiny: *Karma*. "I'm following out my karma," she wrote. "Your karma has taken a bad turn."

I'd like to go to sleep, but what's the point? People will be getting up soon. Vicky's alarm will go off before much longer. I wish I could go upstairs and get back in bed with my wife, tell her I'm sorry, there's been a mistake, let's forget all this – then go to sleep and wake up with her in my arms. But I've forfeited that right. I'm outside all that now, and I can't get back inside! But say I did that. Say I went upstairs and slid into bed with Vicky as I'd like to do. She might wake up and say, *You bastard. Don't you dare touch me, son of a bitch.*

What's she talking about, anyway? I wouldn't touch her. Not in that way, I wouldn't.

After I left Molly, after I'd pulled out on her, about two months after, then Molly really did it. She had her real collapse then, the one that'd been coming on. Her sister saw to it that she got the care she needed. What am I saying? *They put her away.* They had to, they said. They put my wife away. By then I was living with Vicky, and trying not to drink whisky. I couldn't do anything for Molly. I mean, she was there, I was here, and I couldn't have gotten her out of that place if I'd wanted to. But the fact is, I didn't want to. She was in there, they said, because she *needed* to be in there. Nobody said anything about destiny. Things had gone beyond that.

And I didn't even go visit her – not once! At the time, I

didn't think I could stand seeing her in there. But, Christ, what was I? A fair-weather friend? We'd been through plenty. But what on earth would I have said to her? *I'm sorry about all this, honey.* I could have said that, I guess. I intended to write, but I didn't. Not a word. Anyway, when you get right down to it, what could I have said in a letter? *How are they treating you, baby? I'm sorry you're where you are, but don't give up. Remember all the good times? Remember when we were happy together? Hey, I'm sorry they've done this to you. I'm sorry it turned out this way. I'm sorry everything is just garbage now.* I'm sorry, Molly.

I didn't write. I think I was trying to forget about her, to pretend she didn't exist. Molly who?

I left my wife and took somebody else's: Vicky. Now I think maybe I've lost Vicky, too. But Vicky won't be going away to any summer camp for the mentally disabled. She's a hard case. She left her former husband, Joe Kraft, and didn't bat an eye; I don't think she ever lost a night's sleep over it.

Vicky Kraft-Hughes. Amanda Porter. This is where my destiny has brought me? To this street in this neighbourhood, messing up the lives of these women?

Amanda's kitchen light went off when I wasn't looking. The room that was there is gone now, like the others. Only the porch light is still burning. Amanda must have forgotten it, I guess. Hey, Amanda.

Once, when Molly was away in that place and I wasn't in my right mind – let's face it, I was crazy too – one night I was at my friend Alfredo's house, a bunch of us drinking and listening to records. I didn't care any longer what happened to me. Everything, I thought, that could happen had happened. I felt unbalanced. I felt lost. Anyway, there I was at Alfredo's. His paintings of tropical birds and animals hung on every wall in his house, and there were paintings standing around in the

rooms, leaning against things – table-legs, say, or his brick-
and-board bookcase, as well as being stacked on his back
porch. The kitchen served as his studio, and I was sitting at
the kitchen table with a drink in front of me. An easel stood
off to one side in front of the window that overlooked the
alley, and there were crumpled tubes of paint, a palette, and
some brushes lying at one end of the table. Alfredo was
making himself a drink at the counter a few feet away. I loved
the shabby economy of that little room. The stereo music that
came from the living room was turned up, filling the house
with so much sound the kitchen windows rattled in their
frames. Suddenly I began to shake. First my hands began to
shake, and then my arms and shoulders, too. My teeth started
to chatter. I couldn't hold the glass.

"What's going on, man?" Alfredo said, when he turned
and saw the state I was in. "Hey, what is it? What's going on
with you?"

I couldn't tell him. What could I say? I thought I was having
some kind of an attack. I managed to raise my shoulders and
let them drop.

Then Alfredo came over, took a chair and sat down beside
me at the kitchen table. He put his big painter's hand on my
shoulder. I went on shaking. He could feel me shaking.

"What's wrong with you, man? I'm real sorry about everything, man. I know it's real hard right now." Then he said
he was going to fix *menudo* for me. He said it would be good
for what ailed me. "Help your nerves, man," he said. "Calm
you right down." He had all the ingredients for *menudo*, he
said, and he'd been wanting to make some anyway.

"You listen to me. Listen to what I say, man. I'm your
family now," Alfredo said.

It was two in the morning, we were drunk, there were
these other drunk people in the house and the stereo was
going full blast. But Alfredo went to his fridge and opened it
and took some stuff out. He closed the fridge door and looked

in his freezer compartment. He found something in a package. Then he looked around in his cupboards. He took a big pan from the cabinet under the sink, and he was ready.

Tripe. He started with tripe and about a gallon of water. Then he chopped onions and added them to the water, which had started to boil. He put *chorizo* sausage in the pot. After that, he dropped peppercorns into the boiling water and sprinkled in some chilli powder. Then came the olive oil. He opened a big can of tomato sauce and poured that in. He added cloves of garlic, some slices of white bread, salt, and lemon juice. He opened another can – it was hominy – and poured that in the pot, too. He put it all in, and then he turned the heat down and put a lid on the pot.

I watched him. I sat there shaking while Alfredo stood at the stove making *menudo*, talking – I didn't have any idea what he was saying – and, from time to time, he'd shake his head, or else start whistling to himself. Now and then people drifted into the kitchen for beer. But all the while Alfredo went on very seriously looking after his *menudo*. He could have been home, in Morelia, making *menudo* for his family on New Year's Day.

People hung around in the kitchen for a while, joking, but Alfredo didn't joke back when they kidded him about cooking *menudo* in the middle of the night. Pretty soon they left us alone. Finally, while Alfredo stood at the stove with a spoon in his hand, watching me, I got up slowly from the table. I walked out of the kitchen into the bathroom, and then opened another door off the bathroom to the spare room – where I lay down on the bed and fell asleep. When I woke it was mid-afternoon. The *menudo* was gone. The pot was in the sink, soaking. Those other people must have eaten it! They must have eaten it and grown calm. Everyone was gone, and the house was quiet.

I never saw Alfredo more than once or twice afterwards. After that night, our lives took us in separate directions. And those other people who were there – who knows where they went? I'll probably die without ever tasting *menudo*. But who can say?

Is this what it all comes down to then? A middle-aged man involved with his neighbour's wife, linked to an angry ultimatum? What kind of destiny is that? A week, Oliver said. Three or four days now.

A car passes outside with its lights on. The sky is turning grey, and I hear some birds starting up. I decide I can't wait any longer. I can't just sit here, doing nothing – that's all there is to it. I can't keep waiting. I've waited and waited and where's it gotten me? Vicky's alarm will go off soon, Beth will get up and dress for school, Amanda will wake up, too. The entire neighbourhood.

On the back porch I find some old jeans and a sweatshirt, and I change out of my pyjamas. Then I put on my white canvas shoes – "wino" shoes, Alfredo would have called them. Alfredo, where are you?

I go outside to the garage and find the rake and some lawn bags. By the time I get around to the front of the house with the rake, ready to begin, I feel I don't have a choice in the matter any longer. It's light out – light enough at any rate for what I have to do. And then, without thinking about it any more, I start to rake. I rake our yard, every inch of it. It's important it be done right, too. I set the rake right down into the turf and pull hard. It must feel to the grass like it does whenever someone gives your hair a hard jerk. Now and then a car passes in the street and slows, but I don't look up from my work. I know what the people in the cars must be thinking, but they're dead wrong – they don't know the half of it. How could they? I'm happy, raking.

I finish our yard and put the bag out next to the curb. Then I begin next door on the Baxters' yard. In a few minutes Mrs

Baxter comes out on her porch, wearing her bathrobe. I don't acknowledge her. I'm not embarrassed, and I don't want to appear unfriendly. I just want to keep on with what I'm doing.

She doesn't say anything for a while, and then she says, "Good morning, Mr Hughes. How are you this morning?"

I stop what I'm doing and run my arm across my forehead. "I'll be through in a little while," I say. "I hope you don't mind."

"We don't mind," Mrs Baxter says. "Go right ahead, I guess." I see Mr Baxter standing in the doorway behind her. He's already dressed for work in his slacks and sports coat and tie. But he doesn't venture on to the porch. Then Mrs Baxter turns and looks at Mr Baxter, who shrugs.

It's OK, I've finished here anyway. There are other yards, more important yards for that matter. I kneel, and, taking a grip low down on the rake handle, I pull the last of the leaves into my bag and tie off the top. Then, I can't help it, I just stay there, kneeling on the grass with the rake in my hand. When I look up, I see the Baxters come down the porch steps together and move slowly towards me through the wet, sweet-smelling grass. They stop a few feet away and look at me closely.

"There now," I hear Mrs Baxter say. She's still in her robe and slippers. It's nippy out; she holds her robe at the throat. "You did a real fine job for us, yes, you did."

I don't say anything. I don't even say, "You're welcome."

They stand in front of me a while longer, and none of us says anything more. It's as if we've come to an agreement on something. In a minute, they turn around and go back to their house. High over my head, in the branches of the old maple – the place where these leaves come from – birds call out to each other. At least I think they're calling to each other.

Suddenly a car door slams. Mr Baxter is in his car in the drive with the window rolled down. Mrs Baxter says something to him from the front porch which causes Mr

70

Baxter to nod slowly and turn his head in my direction. He sees me kneeling there with the rake, and a look crosses his face. He frowns. In his better moments, Mr Baxter is a decent, ordinary guy – a guy you wouldn't mistake for anyone special. But he *is* special. In my book, he is. For one thing he has a full night's sleep behind him, and he's just embraced his wife before leaving for work. But even before he goes, he's already expected home a set number of hours later. True, in the grander scheme of things, his return will be an event of small moment – but an event nonetheless.

Baxter starts his car and races the engine. Then he backs effortlessly out of the drive, brakes, and changes gears. As he passes on the street, he slows and looks briefly in my direction. He lifts his hand off the steering wheel. It could be a salute or a sign of dismissal. It's a sign, in any case. And then he looks away towards the city. I get up and raise my hand, too – not a wave, exactly, but close to it. Some other cars drive past. One of the drivers must think he knows me because he gives his horn a friendly little tap. I look both ways and then cross the street.

Elephant

I knew it was a mistake to let my brother have the money. I didn't need anybody else owing me. But when he called and said he couldn't make the payment on his house, what could I do? I'd never been inside his house – he lived a thousand miles away, in California; I'd never even *seen* his house – but I didn't want him to lose it. He cried over the phone and said he was losing everything he'd worked for. He said he'd pay me back. February, he said. Maybe sooner. No later, anyway, than March. He said his income-tax refund was on the way. Plus, he said, he had a little investment that would mature in February. He acted secretive about the investment thing, so I didn't press for details.

"Trust me on this," he said. "I won't let you down."

He'd lost his job last July, when the company he worked for, a fibreglass-insulation plant, decided to lay off two hundred employees. He'd been living on his unemployment since then, but now the unemployment was gone, and his savings were gone, too. And he didn't have health insurance any longer. When his job went, the insurance went. His wife, who was ten years older, was diabetic and needed treatment. He'd had to sell the other car – her car, an old station wagon – and a week ago he'd pawned his TV. He told me he'd hurt his back carrying the TV up and down the street where the pawnshops did business. He went from place to place, he said, trying to get the best offer. Somebody finally gave him a hundred dollars for it, this big Sony TV. He told me about the TV, and then about throwing his back out, as if this ought to cinch it with me, unless I had a stone in place of a heart.

"I've gone belly up," he said. "But you can help me pull out of it."

"How much?" I said.

"Five hundred. I could use more, sure, who couldn't?" he said. "But I want to be realistic. I can pay back five hundred. More than that, I'll tell you the truth, I'm not so sure. Brother, I hate to ask. But you're my last resort. Irma Jean and I are going to be on the street before long. I won't let you down," he said. That's what he said. Those were his exact words.

We talked a little more – mostly about our mother and her problems – but, to make a long story short, I sent him the money. I had to. I felt I had to, at any rate – which amounts to the same thing. I wrote him a letter when I sent the cheque and said he should pay the money back to our mother, who lived in the same town he lived in and who was poor and greedy. I'd been mailing cheques to her every month, rain or shine, for three years. But I was thinking that if he paid her the money he owed me it might take me off the hook there and let me breathe for a while. I wouldn't have to worry on that score for a couple of months, anyway. Also, and this is the truth, I thought maybe he'd be more likely to pay her, since they lived right there in the same town and he saw her from time to time. All I was doing was trying to cover myself some way. The thing is, he might have the best intentions of paying me back, but things happen sometimes. Things get in the way of best intentions. Out of sight, out of mind, as they say. But he wouldn't stiff his own mother. Nobody would do that.

I spent hours writing letters, trying to make sure everybody knew what could be expected and what was required. I even phoned out there to my mother several times, trying to explain it to her. But she was suspicious over the whole deal.

74

I went through it with her on the phone step by step, but she was still suspicious. I told her the money that was supposed to come from me on the first of March and on the first of April would instead come from Billy, who owed the money to me. She'd get her money, and she didn't have to worry. The only difference was that Billy would pay it to her those two months instead of me. He'd pay her the money I'd normally be sending to her, but instead of him mailing it to me and then me having to turn around and send it to her he'd pay it to her directly. On any account, she didn't have to worry. She'd get her money, but for those two months it'd come from him – from the money he owed me. My God, I don't know how much I spent on phone calls. And I wish I had fifty cents for every letter I wrote, telling him what I'd told her and telling her what to expect from him – that sort of thing.

But my mother didn't trust Billy. "What if he can't come up with it?" she said to me over the phone. "What then? He's in bad shape, and I'm sorry for him," she said. "But, son, what I want to know is, what if he isn't able to pay me? What if he can't? Then what?"

"Then I'll pay you myself," I said. "Just like always. If he doesn't pay you, I'll pay you. But he'll pay you. Don't worry. He says he will, and he will."

"I don't want to worry," she said. "But I worry anyway. I worry about my boys, and after that I worry about myself. I never thought I'd see one of my boys in this shape. I'm just glad your dad isn't alive to see it."

In three months my brother gave her fifty dollars of what he owed me and was supposed to pay to her. Or maybe it was seventy-five dollars he gave her. There are conflicting stories – two conflicting stories, his and hers. But that's all he paid her of the five hundred – fifty dollars or else seventy-five dollars, according to whose story you want to listen to. I had to make up the rest to her. I had to keep shelling out, same as always. My brother was finished. That's what he told me – that he was finished – when I called to see what was up, after my mother had phoned, looking for her money.

My mother said, "I made the mailman go back and check inside his truck, to see if your letter might have fallen down behind the seat. Then I went around and asked the neighbours did they get any of my mail by mistake. I'm going crazy with worry about this situation, honey." Then she said, "What's a mother supposed to think?" Who was looking out for her best interests in this busines? She wanted to know that, and she wanted to know when she could expect her money.

So that's when I got on the phone to my brother to see if this was just a simple delay or a full-fledged collapse. But, according to Billy, he was a goner. He was absolutely done for. He was putting his house on the market immediately. He just hoped he hadn't waited too long to try and move it. And there wasn't anything left inside the house that he could sell. He'd sold off everything except the kitchen table and chairs. "I wish I could sell my blood," he said. "But who'd buy it? With my luck, I probably have an incurable disease." And, naturally, the investment thing hadn't worked out. When I asked him about it over the phone, all he said was that it hadn't materialized. His tax refund didn't make it, either – the IRS had some kind of lien on his return. "When it rains it pours," he said. "I'm sorry, brother. I didn't mean for this to happen."

"I understand," I said. And I did. But it didn't make it any easier. Anyway, one thing and the other, I didn't get my money from him, and neither did my mother. I had to keep on sending her money every month.

I was sore, yes. Who wouldn't be? My heart went out to him, and I wished trouble hadn't knocked on his door. But my own back was against the wall now. At least, though, whatever happens to him from here on, he won't come back to me for more money – seeing as how he still owes me. Nobody would do that to you. That's how I figured, anyway. But that's how little I knew.

I kept my nose to the grindstone. I got up early every morning and went to work and worked hard all day. When I came home I plopped into the big chair and just sat there. I was so tired it took me a while to get around to unlacing my shoes. Then I just went on sitting there. I was too tired to even get up and turn on the TV.

I was sorry about my brother's troubles. But I had troubles of my own. In addition to my mother, I had several other people on my payroll. I had a former wife I was sending money to every month. I had to do that. I didn't want to, but the court said I had to. And I had a daughter with two kids in Bellingham, and I had to send her something every month. Her kids had to eat, didn't they? She was living with a swine who wouldn't even *look* for work, a guy who couldn't hold a job if they handed him one. The time or two he did find something, he overslept, or his car broke down on the way in to work, or else he'd just be let go, no explanation, and that was that.

Once, long ago, when I used to think like a man about these things, I threatened to kill that guy. But that's neither here nor there. Besides, I was drinking in those days. In any case, the bastard is still hanging around.

My daughter would write these letters and say how they were living on oatmeal, she and her kids. (I guess he was starving, too, but she knew better than to mention that guy's name in her letters to me.) She'd tell me that if I could just carry her until summer things would pick up for her. Things would turn around for her, she was sure, in the summer. If nothing else worked out – but she was sure it would; she had several irons in the fire – she could always get a job in the fish cannery that was not far from where she lived. She'd wear rubber boots and rubber clothes and gloves and pack salmon into cans. Or else she might sell root beer from a vending stand beside the road to people who lined up in their cars at the border, waiting to get into Canada. People sitting in their cars in the middle of summer were going to be thirsty, right? They were going to be crying out for cold drinks. Anyway, one thing or the other, whatever line of work she decided on, she'd do fine in the summer. She just had to make it until then, and that's where I came in.

My daughter said she knew she had to change her life. She wanted to stand on her own two feet like everyone else. She wanted to quit looking at herself as a victim. "I'm not a victim," she said to me over the phone one night. "I'm just a young woman with two kids and a son-of-a-bitch bum who lives with me. No different from lots of other women. I'm not afraid of hard work. Just give me a chance. That's all I ask of the world." She said she could do without for herself. But until her break came, until opportunity knocked, it was the kids she worried about. The kids were always asking her when Grandpop was going to visit, she said. Right this minute they were drawing pictures of the swing sets and swimming pool at the motel I'd stayed in when I'd visited a year ago. But summer was the thing, she said. If she could make it until summer, her troubles would be over. Things would change then – she knew they would. And with a little help from me she could make it. "I don't know what I'd do without you, Dad." That's what she said. It nearly broke my heart. Sure I had to help her. I was glad to be even halfway in a position to help her. I had a job, didn't I? Compared to her and everyone else in my family, I had it made. Compared to the rest, I lived on Easy Street.

I sent the money she asked for. I sent money every time she asked. And then I told her I thought it'd be simpler if I just sent a sum of money, not a whole lot, but money even so, on the first of each month. It would be money she could count on, and it would be *her* money, no one else's – hers and the kids'. That's what I hoped for, anyway. I wished there was some way I could be sure the bastard who lived with her couldn't get his hands on so much as an orange or a piece of bread that my money bought. But I couldn't. I just had to go ahead and send the money and stop worrying about whether he'd soon be tucking into a plate of my eggs and biscuits.

My mother and my daughter and my former wife. That's three people on the payroll right there, not counting my brother. But my son needed money, too. After he graduated from high school, he packed his things, left his mother's house, and went to a college back East. A college in New Hampshire of all places. Who's ever heard of New Hampshire? But he was the first kid in the family on either side of the family, to even *want* to go to college, so everbody thought it was a good idea. I thought so, too, at first. How'd I know it was going to wind up costing me an arm and a leg? He borrowed left and right from the banks to keep himself going. He didn't want to have to work a job and go to school at the same time. That's what he said. And, sure, I guess I can understand it. In a way, I can even sympathize. Who likes to work? I don't. But after he'd borrowed everything he could, everything in sight, including enough to finance a junior year in Germany, I had to begin sending him money, and a lot of it. When, finally, I said I couldn't send any more, he wrote back and said if that was the case, if that was really the way I felt, he was going to deal drugs or else rob a bank – whatever he had to do to get money to live on. I'd be lucky if he wasn't shot or sent to prison.

I wrote back and said I'd changed my mind and I could send him a little more after all. What else could I do? I didn't want his blood on my hands. I didn't want to think of my kid being packed off to prison, or something even worse. I had plenty on my conscience as it was.

That's four people, right? Not counting my brother, who wasn't a regular yet. I was going crazy with it. I worried night and day. I couldn't sleep over it. I was paying out nearly as much money every month as I was bringing in. You don't have to be a genius, or know anything about economics, to understand that this state of affairs couldn't keep on. I had to get a loan to keep up my end of things. That was another monthly payment.

So I started cutting back. I had to quit eating out, for instance. Since I lived alone, eating out was something I liked to do, but it became a thing of the past. And I had to watch myself when it came to thinking about movies. I couldn't buy clothes or get my teeth fixed. The car was falling apart. I needed new shoes, but forget it.

Once in a while I'd get fed up with it and write letters to all of them, threatening to change my name and telling them I was going to quit my job. I'd tell them I was planning a move to Australia. And the thing was, I was serious when I'd say that about Australia, even though I didn't know the first thing about Australia. I just knew it was on the other side of the world, and that's where I wanted to be.

But when it came right down to it, none of them really believed I'd go to Australia. They had me, and they knew it. They knew I was desperate, and they were sorry and they said so. But they counted on it all blowing over before the first of the month, when I had to sit down and make out the cheques.

After one of my letters where I talked about moving to Australia, my mother wrote that she didn't want to be a burden any longer. Just as soon as the swelling went down in her legs, she said, she was going out to look for work. She was seventy-five years old, but maybe she could go back to waitressing, she said. I wrote her back and told her not to be silly. I said I was glad I could help her. And I was. I was glad I could help. I just needed to win the lottery.

My daughter knew Australia was just a way of saying to everybody that I'd had it. She knew I needed a break and something to cheer me up. So she wrote that she was going to leave her kids with somebody and take the cannery job when the season rolled around. She was young and strong, she said. She thought she could work the twelve-to-fourteen-hour-a-day shifts, seven days a week, no problem. She'd just have to tell herself she could do it, get herself psyched up for it, and her body would listen. She just had to line up the right kind of babysitter. That'd be the big thing. It was going to require a special kind of sitter, seeing as how the hours would be long and the kids were hyper to begin with, because of all the Popsicles and Tootsie Rolls, M&Ms, and the like that they put away every day. It's the stuff kids like to eat, right? Anyway, she thought she could find the right person if she kept looking. But she had to buy the boots and clothes for the work, and that's where I could help.

My son wrote that he was sorry for his part in things and thought he and I would both be better off if he ended it once and for all. For one thing, he'd discovered he was allergic to cocaine. It made his eyes stream and affected his breathing, he said. This meant he couldn't test the drugs in the trans-actions he'd need to make. So, before it could even begin, his career as a drug dealer was over. No, he said, better a bullet in the temple and end it all right here. Or maybe hanging. That would save him the trouble of borrowing a gun. And save us the price of bullets. That's actually what he said in his letter, if you can believe it. He enclosed a picture of himself that somebody had taken last summer when he was in the study-abroad programme in Germany. He was standing un-der a big tree with thick limbs hanging down a few feet over his head. In the picture, he wasn't smiling.

My former wife didn't have anything to say on the matter. She didn't have to. She knew she'd get her money the first of each month, even if it had to come all the way from Sydney.

If she didn't get it, she just had to pick up the phone and call her lawyer.

This is where things stood when my brother called one Sunday afternoon in early May. I had the windows open, and a nice breeze moved through the house. The radio was playing. The hillside behind the house was in bloom. But I began to sweat when I heard his voice on the line. I hadn't heard from him since the dispute over the five hundred, so I couldn't believe he was going to try and touch me for more money now. But I began to sweat anyway. He asked how things stood with me, and I launched into the payroll thing and all. I talked about oatmeal, cocaine, fish canneries, suicide, bank jobs, and how I couldn't go to the movies or eat out. I said I had a hole in my shoe. I talked about the payments that went on and on to my former wife. He knew all about this, of course. He knew everything I was telling him. Still, he said he was sorry to hear it. I kept talking. It was his dime. But as he talked I started thinking, *How are you going to pay for this call, Billy?* Then it came to me that *I* was going to pay for it. It was only a matter of minutes, or seconds, until it was all decided.

I looked out the window. The sky was blue, with a few white clouds in it. Some birds clung to a telephone wire. I wiped my face on my sleeve. I didn't know what else I could say. So I suddenly stopped talking and just stared out the window at the mountains, and waited. And that's when my brother said, "I hate to ask you this, but –" When he said that, my heart did this sinking thing. And then he went ahead and asked.

This time it was a thousand. A thousand! He was worse off than when he'd called that other time. He let me have some details. The bill collectors were at the door – the door! he said – and the windows rattled, the house shook, when they hammered with their fists. *Blam, blam, blam,* he said. There was no place to hide from them. His house was about to be pulled out from under him. "Help me, brother," he said.

Where was I going to raise a thousand dollars? I took a good grip on the receiver, turned away from the window, and said, "But you didn't pay me back the last time you borrowed money. What about that?"

"I didn't?" he said, acting surprised. "I guess I thought I had. I wanted to, anyway. I tried to, so help me God."

"You were supposed to pay that money to Mom," I said. "But you didn't. I had to keep giving her money every month, same as always. There's no end to it, Billy. Listen, I take one step forward and I go two steps back. I'm going under. You're all going under, and you're pulling me down with you."

"I paid her *some* of it," he said. "I did pay her a little. Just for the record," he said. "I paid her something."

"She said you gave her fifty dollars and that was all."

"No," he said, "I gave her seventy-five. She forgot about the other twenty-five. I was over there one afternoon, and I gave her two tens and a five. I gave her some cash, and she just forgot about it. Her memory's going. Look," he said, "I promise I'll be good for it this time, I swear to God. Add up what I still owe you and add it to this money here I'm trying to borrow, and I'll send you a cheque. We'll exchange cheques. Hold on to my cheque for two months, that's all I'm asking. I'll be out of the woods in two months' time. Then you'll have your money. July 1st, I promise, no later, and this time I *can* swear to it. We're in the process of selling this little piece of property that Irma Jean inherited a while back from her uncle. It's as good as sold. The deal has closed. It's just a question now of working out a couple of minor details and signing the papers. Plus, I've got this job lined up. It's definite. I'll have to drive fifty miles round trip every day, but that's no problem – hell, no. I'd drive a hundred and fifty if I had to, and be glad to do it. I'm saying I'll have money in the bank in two months' time. You'll get your money, all of it, by July 1st, and you can count on it."

"Billy, I love you," I said. "But I've got a load to carry. I'm carrying a very heavy load these days, in case you didn't know."

"That's why I won't let you down on this," he said. "You have my word of honour. You can trust me on this absolutely. I promise you my cheque will be good in two months, no later. Two months is all I'm asking for. Brother, I don't know where else to turn. You're my last hope."

I did it, sure. To my surprise, I still had some credit with the bank, so I borrowed the money, and I sent it to him. Our cheques crossed in the mail. I stuck a thumbtack through his cheque and put it up on the kitchen wall next to the calendar and the picture of my son standing under that tree. And then I waited.

I kept waiting. My brother wrote and asked me not to cash the cheque on the day we'd agreed to. Please wait a while longer is what he said. Some things had come up. The job he'd been promised had fallen through at the last minute. That was one thing that came up. And that little piece of property belonging to his wife hadn't sold after all. At the last minute she'd had a change of heart about selling it. It had been in her family for generations. What could he do? It was her land, and she wouldn't listen to reason, he said.

My daughter telephoned around this time to say that some-body had broken into her trailer and ripped her off. Every-thing in the trailer. Every stick of furniture was gone when she came home from work after her first night at the cannery. There wasn't even a chair for her to sit down on. Her bed had been stolen, too. They were going to have to sleep on the floor like gypsies, she said.

"Where was what's-his-name when this happened?" I said.

She said he'd been out looking for work earlier in the day. She guessed he was with friends. Actually, she didn't know his whereabouts at the time of the crime, or even right now, for that matter. "I hope he's at the bottom of the river," she said. The kids had been with the sitter when the rip-off happened. But, anyway, if she could just borrow enough from me to buy some secondhand furniture she'd pay me back, she said, when she got her first cheque. If she had some money from me before the end of the week – I could wire it, maybe – she could pick up some essentials. "Somebody's violated my space," she said. "I feel like I've been raped."

My son wrote from New Hampshire that it was essential he go back to Europe. His life hung in the balance, he said. He was graduating at the end of summer session, but he couldn't stand to live in America a day longer after that. This was a materialist society, and he simply couldn't take it any more. People over here, in the US, couldn't hold a conversation unless *money* figured in it some way, and he was sick of it. He wasn't a Yuppie, and didn't want to become a Yuppie. That wasn't his thing. He'd get out of my hair, he said, if he could just borrow enough from me, this one last time, to buy a ticket Germany.

I didn't hear anything from my former wife. I didn't have to. We both knew how things stood there.

My mother wrote that she was having to do without support hose and wasn't able to have her hair tinted. She'd thought this would be the year she could put some money back for the rainy days ahead, but it wasn't working out that way. She could see it wasn't in the cards. "How are you?" she wanted to know. "How's everybody else? I hope you're OK."

I put more cheques in the mail. Then I held my breath and waited.

While I was waiting, I had this dream one night. Two dreams, really. I dreamt them on the same night. In the first dream, my dad was alive once more, and he was giving me a ride on his shoulders. I was this little kid, maybe five or six years old. *Get up here,* he said, and he took me by the hands and swung me on to his shoulders. I was high off the ground, but I wasn't afraid. He was holding on to me. We were holding on to each other. Then he began to move down the sidewalk. I brought my hands up from his shoulders and put them around his forehead. *Don't muss my hair,* he said. *You can let go,* he said, *I've got you. You won't fall.* When he said, that, I became aware of the strong grip of his hands around my ankles. Then I did let go. I turned loose and held my arms out on either side of me. I kept them out there like that for balance. My dad went on walking while I rode on his shoulders. I pretended he was an elephant. I don't know where we were going. Maybe we were going to the store, or else to the park so he could push me in the swing.

I woke up then, got out of bed, and used the bathroom. It was starting to get light out, and it was only an hour or so until I had to get up. I thought about making coffee and getting dressed. But then I decided to go back to bed. I didn't plan to sleep, though. I thought I'd just lie there for a while with my hands behind my neck and watch it turn light out and maybe think about my dad a little, since I hadn't thought about him in a long time. He just wasn't a part of my life any longer, waking or sleeping. Anyway, I got back in bed. But it couldn't have been more than a minute before I fell asleep once more, and when I did I got into this other dream. My former wife was in it, though she wasn't my former wife in the dream. She was still my wife. My kids were in it, too. They were little, and they were eating potato chips. In my dream, I thought I could smell the potato chips and hear them being eaten. We were on a blanket, and we were close to some water. There was a sense of satisfaction and well-being in the dream. Then, suddenly, I found myself in the company of some other people – people I didn't know – and the next thing that happened was that I was kicking the window out of my son's car and threatening his life, as I did once, a long time ago. He was inside the car as my shoe smashed through the glass. That's when my eyes flew open, and I woke up. The alarm was going off. I reached over and pushed the switch and lay there for a few minutes more, my heart racing. In the second dream, somebody had offered me some whisky, and I drank it. Drinking that whisky was the thing that scared me. That was the worst thing that could have happened. That was rock bottom. Compared to that, everything else was a picnic. I lay there for a minute longer, trying to calm down. Then I got up.

I made coffee and sat at the kitchen table in front of the window. I pushed my cup back and forth in little circles on the table and began to think seriously about Australia again. And then, all of a sudden, I could imagine how it must have sounded to my family when I'd threatened them with a move to Australia. They would have been shocked at first, and even a little scared. Then, because they knew me, they'd probably started laughing. Now, thinking about their laughter, I had to laugh, too. *Ha, ha, ha.* That was exactly the sound I made there at the table – *ha, ha, ha* – as if I'd read somewhere how to laugh.

What was it I planned to do in Australia, anyway? The truth was, I wouldn't be going there any more than I'd be going to Timbuktu, the moon, or the North Pole. Hell, I didn't want to go to Australia. But once I understood this, once I understood I wouldn't be going there – or anywhere else, for that matter – I began to feel better. I lit another cigarette and poured some more coffee. There wasn't any milk for the coffee, but I didn't care. I could skip having milk in my coffee for a day and it wouldn't kill me. Pretty soon I packed the lunch and filled the thermos and put the thermos in the lunch pail. Then I went outside.

It was a fine morning. The sun lay over the mountains behind the town, and a flock of birds was moving from one part of the valley to another. I didn't bother to lock the door. I remembered what had happened to my daughter, but decided I didn't have anything worth stealing anyway. There was nothing in the house I couldn't live without. I had the TV, but I was sick of watching TV. They'd be doing me a favour if they broke in and took it off my hands.

I felt pretty good, all things considered, and I decided to walk to work. It wasn't all that far, and I had time to spare. I'd save a little gas, sure, but that wasn't the main consideration. It was summer, after all, and before long summer would be over. Summer, I couldn't help thinking, had been the time everybody's luck had been going to change.

I started walking alongside the road, and it was then, for some reason, I began to think about my son. I wished him well, wherever he was. If he'd made it back to Germany by now – and he should have – I hoped he was happy. He hadn't written yet to give me his address, but I was sure I'd hear something before long. And my daughter, God love her and keep her. I hoped she was doing OK. I decided to write her a letter that evening and tell her I was rooting for her. My mother was alive and more or less in good health, and I felt lucky there, too. If all went well, I'd have her for several more years.

Birds were calling, and some cars passed me on the highway. Good luck to you, too, brother, I thought. I hope your ship comes in. Pay me back when you get it. And my former wife, the woman I used to love so much. She was alive, and she was well, too – so far as I knew, anyway. I wished her happiness. When all was said and done, I decided things could be a lot worse. Just now, of course, things were hard for everyone. People's luck had gone south on them was all. But things were bound to change soon. Things would pick up in the fall maybe. There was lots to hope for.

I kept on walking. Then I began to whistle. I felt I had the right to whistle if I wanted to. I let my arms swing as I walked. But the lunch pail kept throwing me off balance. I had sandwiches, an apple, and some cookies in there, not to mention the thermos. I stopped in front of Smitty's, an old café that had gravel in the parking area and boards over the windows. The place had been boarded up for as long as I could remember. I decided to put the lunch pail down for a minute. I did that, and then I raised my arms – raised them up level with my shoulders. I was standing there like that, like a goof, when somebody tooted a car horn and pulled off the highway into the parking area. I picked up my lunch pail and went over to the car. It was a guy I knew from work whose name was George. He reached over and opened the door on the passenger's side. "Hey, get in, buddy," he said.

"Hello, George," I said. I got in and shut the door, and the car sped off, throwing gravel from under the tyres.

"I saw you," George said. "Yeah, I did, I saw you. You're in training for something, but I don't know what." He looked at me and then looked at the road again. He was going fast. "You always walk down the road with your arms out like that?" He laughed – *ha, ha, ha* – and stepped on the gas.

"Sometimes," I said. "It depends, I guess. Actually, I was standing," I said. I lit a cigarette and leaned back in the seat.

"So what's new?" George said. He put a cigar in his mouth, but he didn't light it.

"Nothing's new," I said. "What's new with you?"

George shrugged. Then he grinned. He was going very fast now. Wind buffeted the car and whistled by outside the windows. He was driving as if we were late for work. But we weren't late. We had lots of time, and I told him so.

Nevertheless, he cranked it up. We passed the turn-off and kept going. We were moving by then, heading straight towards the mountains. He took the cigar out of his mouth and put it in his shirt pocket. "I borrowed some money and had this baby overhauled," he said. Then he said he wanted me to see something. He punched it and gave it everything he could. I fastened my seat belt and held on.

"Go," I said. "What are you waiting for, George?" And that's when we really flew. Wind howled outside the windows. He had it floored, and we were going flat out. We streaked down that road in his big unpaid-for car.

Blackbird Pie

I was in my room one night when I heard something in the corridor. I looked up from my work and saw an envelope slide under the door. It was a thick envelope, but not so thick it couldn't be pushed under the door. My name was written on the envelope, and what was inside purported to be a letter from my wife. I say "purported" because even though the grievances could only have come from someone who'd spent twenty-three years observing me on an intimate, day-to-day basis, the charges were outrageous and completely out of keeping with my wife's character. Most important, however, the handwriting was not my wife's handwriting. But if it wasn't her handwriting, then whose was it?

I wish now I'd kept the letter, so I could reproduce it down to the last comma, the last uncharitable exclamation point. The tone is what I'm talking about now, not just the content. But I didn't keep it, I'm sorry to say. I lost it, or else misplaced it. Later, after the sorry business I'm about to relate, I was cleaning out my desk and may have accidentally thrown it away – which is uncharacteristic of *me*, since I usually don't throw anything away.

In any case, I have a good memory. I can recall every word of what I read. My memory is such that I used to win prizes in school because of my ability to remember names and dates, inventions, battles, treaties, alliances, and the like. I always scored highest on factual tests, and in later years, in the "real world", as it's called, my memory stood me in good stead. For instance, if I were asked right now to give the details of the Council of Trent or the Treaty of Utrecht, or to talk about Carthage, that city razed by the Romans after Hannibal's defeat (the Roman soldiers ploughed salt into the ground so that Carthage could never be called Carthage again), I could do so. If called upon to talk about the Seven Years' War, the Thirty Years', or the Hundred Years' War, or simply the First Silesian War, I could hold forth with the greatest enthusiasm and confidence. Ask me anything about the Tartars, the Renaissance popes, or the rise and fall of the Ottoman Empire. Thermopylae, Shiloh, or the Maxim gun. Easy. Tannenberg? Simple as blackbird pie. The famous four and twenty that were set before the king. At Agincourt, English longbows carried the day. And here's something else. Everyone has heard of the Battle of Lepanto, the last great sea battle fought in ships powered by galley slaves. This fracas took place in 1571 in the eastern Mediterranean, when the combined naval forces of the Christian nations of Europe turned back the Arab hordes under the infamous Ali Muezzin Zade, a man who was fond of personally cutting of the noses of his prisoners before calling in the executioners. But does anyone remember that Cervantes was involved in this affair and had his left hand lopped off in the battle? Something else. The combined French and Russian losses in one day at Borodino were seventy-five thousand men – the equivalent in fatalities of a fully loaded jumbo jet crashing every three minutes from breakfast to sundown. Kutuzov pulled his forces back towards Moscow. Napoleon drew breath, marshalled his troops, and continued his advance. He entered the downtown area of Moscow, where he stayed for a month waiting for Kutuzov, who never showed his face again. The Russian generalissimo was waiting for snow and ice, for Napoleon to begin his retreat to France.

Things stick in my head. I remember. So when I say I can

re-create the letter – the portion that I read, which catalogues the charges against me – I mean what I say.

In part, the letter went as follows:

Dear,

Things are not good. Things, in fact, are bad. Things have gone from bad to worse. And you know what I'm talking about. We've come to the end of the line. It's over with us. Still, I find myself wishing we could have talked about it.

It's been such a long time now since we've talked. I mean really *talked*. Even after we were married we used to talk and talk, exchanging news and ideas. When the children were little, or even after they were more grown-up, we still found time to talk. It was more difficult then, naturally, but we managed, we found time. We *made* time. We'd have to wait until after they were asleep, or else when they were playing outside, or with a sitter. But we managed. Sometimes we'd engage a sitter just so we *could* talk. On occasion we talked the night away, talked until the sun came up. Well. Things happen, I know. Things change. Bill had that trouble with the police, and Linda found herself pregnant, etc. Our quiet time together flew out the window. And gradually your responsibilities backed up on you. Your work became more important, and our time together was squeezed out. Then, once the children left home, our time for talking was back. We had each other again, only we had less and less to talk about. "It happens," I can hear some wise man saying. And he's right. *It happens*. But it happened to us. In any case, no blame. *No blame*. That's not what this letter is about. *I want to talk about us*. I want to talk about *now*. The time has come, you see, to admit that *the impossible* has happened. To cry *Uncle*. To beg off. To –

93

I read this far and stopped. Something was wrong. Something was fishy in Denmark. The sentiments expressed in the letter may have belonged to my wife. (Maybe they did. Say they did, grant that the sentiments expressed *were* hers.) But the handwriting *was not her handwriting*. And I ought to know. I consider myself an expert in this matter of her handwriting. And yet if it wasn't her handwriting, who on earth *had* written these lines?

I should say a little something about ourselves and our life here. During the time I'm writing about we were living in a house we'd taken for the summer. I'd just recovered from an illness that had set me back in most things I'd hoped to accomplish that spring. We were surrounded on three sides by meadows, birch woods, and some low, rolling hills – a "territorial view", as the realtor had called it when he described it to us over the phone. In front of the house was a lawn that had grown shaggy, owing to lack of interest on my part, and a long gravelled drive that led to the road. Behind the road we could see the distant peaks of mountains. Thus the phrase "territorial view" – having to do with a vista appreciated only at a distance.

My wife had no friends here in the country, and no one came to visit. Frankly, I was glad for the solitude. But she was a woman who was used to having friends, used to dealing with shopkeepers and tradesmen. Out here, it was just the two of us, thrown back on our resources. Once upon a time a house in the country would have been our ideal – we would have *coveted* such an arrangement. Now I can see it wasn't such a good idea. No, it wasn't.

Both our children had left home long ago. Now and then a letter came from one of them. And once in a blue moon, on a holiday, say, one of them might telephone – a collect call, naturally, my wife being only too happy to accept the charges. This seeming indifference on their part was, I believe, a major cause of my wife's sadness and general discontent–a discontent,

I have to admit, I'd been vaguely aware of before our move to the country. In any case, to find herself in the country after so many years of living close to a shopping mall and bus service, with a taxi no farther away than the telephone in the hall – it must have been hard on her, very hard. I think her *decline*, as a historian might put it, was accelerated by our move to the country. I think she slipped a cog after that. I'm speaking from hindsight, of course, which always tends to confirm the obvious.

I don't know what else to say in regard to this matter of the handwriting. How much more can I say and still retain credibility? We were alone in the house. No one else – to my knowledge, anyway – was in the house and could have penned the letter. Yet I remain convinced to this day that it was not her handwriting that covered the pages of the letter. After all, I'd been reading my wife's handwriting since before she was my wife. As far back as what might be called our prehistory days – the time she went away to school as a girl, wearing a grey-and-white school uniform. She wrote letters to me every day that she was away, and she was away for two years, not counting holidays and summer vacations. Altogether, in the course of our relationship, I would estimate (a conservative estimate, too), counting our separations and the short periods of time I was away on business or in the hospital, etc. – I would estimate, as I say, that I received seventeen hundred or possibly eighteen hundred and fifty handwritten letters from her, not to mention hundreds, maybe thousands, more informal notes ("On your way home, please pick up dry cleaning, and some spinach pasta from Corti Bros"). I could recognize her handwriting anywhere in the world. Give me a few words. I'm confident that if I were in Jaffa, or Marrakech, and picked up a note in the marketplace, I would recognize it if it was my wife's handwriting. A word, even. Take this word *"talked"*, for instance. That simply isn't the way she'd write "talked"! Yet I'm the first to admit I don't know *whose* handwriting it is if it isn't hers.

Secondly, my wife *never* underlined her words for empha-
sis. Never. I don't recall a single instance of her doing this –
not once in our entire married life, not to mention the letters
I received from her before we were married. It would be
reasonable enough, I suppose, to point out that it could
happen to anyone. That is, anyone could find himself in a
situation that is completely atypical and, *given the pressure of
the moment*, do something totally out of character and draw a
line, the merest *line*, under a word, or maybe under an entire
sentence.

I would go so far as to say that every word of this entire
letter, so-called (though I haven't read it through in its en-
tirety, and won't, since I can't find it now), is utterly false. I
don't mean false in the sense of "untrue", necessarily. There
is some truth, perhaps, to the charges. I don't want to quibble.
I don't want to appear small in this matter; things are bad
enough already in this department. No. What I want to say,
all I want to say, is that while the sentiments expressed in the
letter may be my wife's, may even hold *some* truth – be
legitimate, so to speak – the force of the accusations levelled
against me is diminished, if not entirely undermined, even
discredited, because she *did not* in fact write the letter. Or, if
she *did* write it, then discredited by the fact that she didn't
write it in her own handwriting! Such evasion is what makes
men hunger for facts. As always, there are some.

On the evening in question, we ate dinner rather silently but
not unpleasantly, as was our custom. From time to time I
looked up and smiled across the table as a way of showing
my gratitude for the delicious meal – poached salmon, fresh
asparagus, rice pilaff with almonds. The radio played softly
in the other room; it was a little suite by Poulenc that I'd first
heard on a digital recording five years before in an apartment
on Van Ness, in San Francisco, during a thunderstorm.

When we'd finished eating, and after we'd had our coffee and dessert, my wife said something that startled me. "Are you planning to be in your room this evening?" she said.

"I am," I said. "What did you have in mind?"

"I simply wanted to know." She picked up her cup and drank some coffee. But she avoided looking at me, even though I tried to catch her eye.

Are you planning to be in your room this evening? Such a question was altogether out of character for her. I wonder now why on earth I didn't pursue this at the time. She knows my habits, if anyone does. But I think her mind was made up even then. I think she was concealing something even as she spoke.

"Of course I'll be in my room this evening," I repeated, perhaps a trifle impatiently. She didn't say anything else, and neither did I. I drank the last of my coffee and cleared my throat.

She glanced up and held my eyes a moment. Then she nodded, as if we had agreed on something. (But we hadn't, of course.) She got up and began to clear the table.

I felt as if dinner had somehow ended on an unsatisfactory note. Something else – a few words maybe – was needed to round things off and put the situation right again.

"There's a fog coming in," I said.

"Is there? I hadn't noticed," she said.

She wiped away a place on the window over the sink with a dish towel and looked out. For a minute she didn't say anything. Then she said – again mysteriously or so it seems to me now – "There is. Yes, it's very foggy. It's a heavy fog, isn't it?" That's all she said. Then she lowered her eyes and began to wash the dishes.

I sat at the table a while longer before I said, "I think I'll go to my room now."

She took her hands out of the water and rested them against

the counter. I thought she might proffer a word or two of encouragement for the work I was engaged in, but she didn't. Not a peep. It was as if she were waiting for me to leave the kitchen so she could enjoy her privacy.

Remember, I was at work in my room at the time the letter was slipped under the door. I read enough to question the handwriting and to wonder how it was that my wife had presumably been busy somewhere in the house and writing me a letter at the same time. Before reading further in the letter, I got up and went over to the door, unlocked it, and checked the corridor.

It was dark at this end of the house. But when I cautiously put my head out I could see light from the living room at the end of the hallway. The radio was playing quietly, as usual. Why did I hesitate? Except for the fog, it was a night very much like any other we had spent together in the house. But there was *something else afoot* tonight. At that moment I found myself afraid – afraid, if you can believe it, in my own house! – to walk down the hall and satisfy myself that all was well. Or if something was wrong, if my wife was experiencing – how should I put it? – difficulties of any sort, hadn't I best confront the situation before letting it go any further, before losing any more time on this stupid business of reading her words in somebody else's handwriting!

But I didn't investigate. Perhaps I wanted to avoid a frontal attack. In any case, I drew back and shut and locked the door before returning to the letter. But I was angry now as I saw the evening sliding away in this foolish and incomprehensible business. I was beginning to feel *uneasy*. (No other word will do.) I could feel my gorge rising as I picked up the letter purporting to be from my wife and once more began to read.

The time has come and gone for us – us, you and me – to put all our cards on the table. Thee and me. Lancelot and Guinevere. Abélard and Héloïse. Troilus and Cressida.

Pyramus and Thisbe. JAJ and Nora Barnacle, etc. You
know what I'm saying, honey. We've been together a long
time – thick and thin, illness and health, stomach distress,
eye-ear-nose-and-throat trouble, high times and low.
Now? Well, I don't know what I can say now except the
truth: I can't go it another step.

At this point, I threw down the letter and went to the door
again, deciding to settle this once and for all. I wanted an
accounting, and I wanted it now. I was, I think, *in a rage*. But
at this point, just as I opened the door, I heard a low murmur-
ing from the living room. It was as if somebody were trying
to say something over the phone and this somebody were
taking pains not to be overheard. Then I heard the receiver
being replaced. Just this. Then everything was *as before* – the
radio playing softly, the house otherwise quiet. But I had
heard a voice.

In place of anger, I began to feel panic. I grew afraid as I
looked down the corridor. Things were the same as before –
the light was on in the the living room, the radio played
softly. I took a few steps and listened. I hoped I might hear
the comforting, rhythmic clicking of her knitting needles, or
the sound of a page being turned, but there was nothing
of the sort. I took a few steps towards the living room and
then – what should I say? – I lost my nerve, or maybe my
curiosity. It was at that moment I heard *the muted sound of a
doorknob being turned*, and afterwards the unmistakable sound
of a door opening and closing quietly.

My impulse was to walk rapidly down the corridor and
into the living room and get to the bottom of this thing once
and for all. But I didn't want to act impulsively and possibly
discredit myself. I'm not impulsive, so I waited. But there
was activity of some sort in the house – something was afoot,
I was sure of it – and of course it was my duty, for my
own peace of mind, not to mention the possible safety and

well-being of my wife, to act. But I didn't. I couldn't. The moment was there, but I hesitated. Suddenly it was too late for any decisive action. The moment had come and gone, and could not be called back. Just so did Darius hesitate and then fail to act at the Battle of Granicus, and the day was lost, Alexander the Great rolling him up on every side and giving him a real walloping.

I went back to my room and closed the door. But *my heart was racing*. I sat in my chair and, trembling, picked up the pages of the letter once more.

But now here's the curious thing. Instead of beginning to read the letter through, from start to finish, or even starting at the point where I'd stopped earlier, I took pages at random and held them under the table lamp, picking out a line here and a line there. This allowed me to juxtapose the charges made against me until the entire indictment (for that's what it was) took on quite another character – one more acceptable, since it had lost its chronology and, with it, a little of its punch.

So. Well. In this manner, going from page to page, here a line, there a line, I read in snatches the following – which might under different circumstances serve as a kind of abstract:

> . . . withdrawing farther into . . . a small enough thing, but . . . talcum powder sprayed over the bathroom, including walls and baseboards . . . a shell . . . not to mention the insane asylum . . . until finally . . . a balanced view . . . the grave. Your "work" . . . Please! Give me a break . . . No one, not even . . . Not another word on the subject! . . . The children . . . but the real issue . . . not to mention the loneliness . . . Jesus H. Christ! Really! I mean . . .

At this point I distinctly heard the front door close. I dropped the pages of the letter on to the desk and hurried to the living room. It didn't take long to see that my wife wasn't in the house. (The house is small – two bedrooms, one of which we refer to as my room or, on occasion, as my study.) But let the record show: *every light in the house was burning.*

A heavy fog lay outside the windows, a fog so dense I could scarcely see the driveway. The porch light was on and a suitcase stood outside on the porch. It was my wife's suitcase, the one she'd brought packed full of her things when we moved here. What on earth was going on? I opened the door. Suddenly – I don't know how to say this other than how it was – a horse stepped out of the fog, and then, an instant later, as I watched, dumbfounded, another horse. These horses were grazing in our front yard. I saw my wife alongside one of the horses, and I called her name.

"Come on out here," she said. "Look at this. Doesn't this beat anything?"

She was standing beside this big horse, patting its flank. She was dressed in her best clothes and had on heels and was wearing a hat. (I hadn't seen her in a hat since her mother's funeral, three years before.) Then she moved forward and put her face against the horse's mane.

"Where did you come from, you big baby?" she said. "Where did you come from, sweetheart?" Then, as I watched, she began to cry into the horse's mane.

"There, there," I said and started down the steps. I went over and patted the horse, and then I touched my wife's shoulder. She drew back. The horse snorted, raised its head a moment, and then went to cropping the grass once more. "What is it?" I said to my wife. "For God's sake, what's happening here, anyway?"

She didn't answer. The horse moved a few steps but continued pulling and eating the grass. The other horse was munching grass as well. My wife moved with the horse, hanging on to its mane. I put my hand against the horse's neck and felt a surge of power run up my arm to the shoulder. I shivered. My wife was still crying. I felt helpless, but I was scared, too.

"Can you tell me what's going on?" I said. "Why are you dressed like this? What's that suitcase doing on the front porch? Where did these horses come from? For God's sake, can you tell me what's happening?"

My wife began to croon to the horse. Croon! Then she stopped and said, "You didn't read my letter, did you? You might have skimmed it, but you didn't read it. Admit it!"

"I did read it," I said. I was lying, yes, but it was a white lie. A partial untruth. But he who is blameless, let him throw out the first stone. "But tell me what is going on anyway," I said.

My wife turned her head from side to side. She pushed her face into the horse's dark wet mane. I could hear the horse *chomp, chomp, chomp*. Then it snorted as it took in air through its nostrils.

She said, "There was this girl, you see. Are you listening? And this girl loved this boy so much. She loved him even more than herself. But the boy – well, he grew up. I don't know what happened to him. Something, anyway. He got cruel without meaning to be cruel and he –"

I didn't catch the rest, because just then a car appeared out of the fog, in the drive, with its headlights on and a flashing blue light on its roof. It was followed, a minute later, by a pick-up truck pulling what looked like a horse trailer, though with the fog it was hard to tell. It could have been anything – a big portable oven, say. The car pulled right up on to the lawn and stopped. Then the pick-up drove alongside the car and stopped, too. Both vehicles kept their headlights on and their engines running, which contributed to the eerie, bizarre aspect of things. A man wearing a cowboy hat – a rancher, I supposed – stepped down from the pick-up. He raised the collar of his sheepskin coat and whistled to the horses. Then a big man in a raincoat got out of the car. He was a much bigger man than the rancher, and he, too, was wearing a cowboy hat. But his raincoat was open, and I could see a pistol strapped to his waist. He had to be a deputy sheriff. Despite everything that was going on, and the anxiety I felt, I found it *worth noting* that both men were wearing hats. I ran my hand through my hair, and was sorry I wasn't wearing a hat of my own.

"I called the sheriff's department a while ago," my wife said. "When I first saw the horses." She waited a minute and then she said something else. "Now you won't need to give me a ride into town after all. I mentioned that in my letter, the letter you read. I said I'd need a ride into town. I can get a ride – at least, I think I can – with one of these gentlemen. And I'm not changing my mind about anything, either. I'm saying this decision is irrevocable. Look at me!" she said.

I'd been watching them round up the horses. The deputy was holding his flashlight while the rancher walked a horse up a little ramp into the trailer. I turned to look at this woman I didn't know any longer.

"I'm leaving you," she said. "That's what's happening. I'm heading for town tonight. I'm striking out on my own. It's all in the letter you read." Whereas, as I said earlier, my wife never underlined words in her letters she was now speaking (having dried her tears) as if virtually every other word out of her mouth ought to be emphasized.

"What's gotten *into* you?" I heard myself say. It was almost as if I couldn't help adding pressure to some of my own words. "Why are you *doing* this?"

She shook her head. The rancher was loading the second horse into the trailer now, whistling sharply, clapping his hands and shouting an occasional "Whoa! Whoa, damn you! Back up now. Back up!"

The deputy came over to us with a clipboard under his

arm. He was holding a big flashlight. "Who called?" he said.

"I did," my wife said.

The deputy looked her over for a minute. He flashed the light on to her high heels and then up to her hat. "You're all dressed up," he said.

"I'm leaving my husband," she said.

The deputy nodded, as if he understood. (But he didn't, he couldn't!) "He's not going to give you any trouble, is he?" the deputy said, shining his light into my face and moving the light up and down rapidly. "You're not, are you?"

"No," I said. "No trouble. But I resent —"

"Good," the deputy said. "Enough said, then."

The rancher closed and latched the door to his trailer. Then he walked towards us through the wet grass, which, I noticed, reached to the tops of his boots.

"I want to thank you folks for calling," he said. "Much obliged. That's one heavy fog. If they'd wandered on to the main road, they could have raised hob out there."

"The lady placed the call," the deputy said. "Frank, she needs a ride into town. She's leaving home. I don't know who the injured party is here, but she's the one leaving." He turned then to my wife. "You sure about this, are you?" he said to her.

She nodded. "I'm sure."

"Okay," the deputy said. "That's settled, anyway. Frank, you listening? I can't drive her to town. I've got another stop to make. So can you help her out and take her into town? She probably wants to go to the bus station or else to the hotel. That's where they usually go. Is that where you want to go to?" the deputy said to my wife. "Frank needs to know."

"He can drop me off at the bus station," my wife said. "That's my suitcase on the porch."

"What about it, Frank?" the deputy said.

"I guess I can, sure," Frank said, taking off his hat and

putting it back on again. "I'd be glad to, I guess. But I don't want to interfere in anything."

"Not in the least," my wife said. "I don't want to be any trouble, but I'm – well, distressed just now. Yes, I'm distressed. But it'll be all right once I'm away from here. Away from this awful place. I'll just check and make doubly sure I haven't left anything behind. Anything *important*," she added. She hesitated and then she said, "This isn't as sudden as it looks. It's been coming for a long, long time. We've been married for a good many years. Good times and bad, up times and down. We've had them all. But it's time I was on my own. Yes, it's time. Do you know what I'm saying, gentlemen?"

Frank took off his hat again and turned it around in his hands as if examining the brim. Then he put it back on his head.

The deputy said, "These things happen. Lord knows none of us is perfect. We weren't made perfect. The only angels is to be found in Heaven."

My wife moved towards the house, picking her way through the wet, shaggy grass in her high heels. She opened the front door and went inside. I could see her moving behind the lighted windows, and something came to me then. *I might never see her again*. That's what crossed my mind, and it staggered me.

The rancher, the deputy, and I stood around waiting, not saying anything. The damp fog drifted between us and the lights from their vehicles. I could hear the horses shifting in the trailer. We were all uncomfortable, I think. But I'm speaking only for myself, of course. I don't know what they felt. Maybe they saw things like this happen every night – saw people's lives flying apart. The deputy did, maybe. But Frank, the rancher, he kept his eyes lowered. He put his hands in his front pockets and then took them out again. He kicked at something in the grass. I folded my arms and went on standing there, not knowing what was going to happen next. The deputy kept turning off his flashlight and then turning it on again. Every so often he'd reach out and swat the fog with it. One of the horses whinnied from the trailer, and then the other horse whinnied, too.

"A fellow can't see anything in this fog," Frank said.

I knew he was saying it to make conversation.

"It's as bad as I've ever seen it," the deputy said. Then he looked over at me. He didn't shine the light in my eyes this time, but he said something. He said, "Why's she leaving you? You hit her or something? Give her a smack, did you?"

"I've never hit her," I said. "Not in all the time we've been married. There was reason enough a few times, but I didn't. She hit me once," I said.

"Now, don't get started," the deputy said. "I don't want to hear any crap tonight. Don't say anything, and there won't be anything. No rough stuff. Don't even think it. There isn't going to be any trouble here tonight, is there?"

The deputy and Frank were watching me. I could tell Frank was embarrassed. He took out his makings and began to roll a cigarette.

"No," I said. "No trouble."

My wife came on to the porch and picked up her suitcase. I had the feeling that not only had she taken a last look around but she'd used the opportunity to freshen herself up, put on new lipstick, etc. The deputy held his flashlight for her as she came down the steps. "Right this way, ma'am," he said. "Watch your step, now – it's slippery."

"I'm ready to go," she said.

"Right," Frank said. "Well, just to make sure we got this all straight now." He took off his hat once more and held it. "I'll carry you into town and I'll drop you off at the bus station. But, you understand, I don't want to be in the middle of something. You know what I mean." He looked at my wife, and then he looked at me.

"That's right," the deputy said. "You said a mouthful. Statistics show that your domestic dispute is, time and again, potentially the most dangerous situation a person, especially a law-enforcement officer, can get himself involved in. But I think this situation is going to be the shining exception. Right, folks?"

My wife looked at me and said, "I don't think I'll kiss you. No, I won't kiss you goodbye. I'll just say so long. Take care of yourself."

"That's right," the deputy said. "Kissing – who knows what that'll lead to, right?" He laughed.

I had the feeling they were all waiting for me to say something. But for the first time in my life I felt at a loss for words. Then I *took heart* and said to my wife, "The last time you wore that hat, you wore a veil with it and I held your arm. You were in mourning for your mother. And you wore a dark dress, not the dress you're wearing tonight. But those are the same high heels, I remember. Don't leave me like this," I said. "I don't know what I'll do."

"I have to," she said. "It's all in the letter – everything's spelled out in the letter. The rest is in the area of – I don't know. Mystery or speculation, I guess. In any case, there's nothing in the letter you don't already know." Then she turned to Frank and said, "Let's go, Frank. I can call you Frank, can't I?"

"Call him anything you want," the deputy said, "long as you call him in time for supper." He laughed again – a big, hearty laugh.

"Right," Frank said. "Sure you can. Well, OK. Let's go, then." He took the suitcase from my wife and went over to his pick-up and put the suitcase into the cab. Then he stood by the door on the passenger's side, holding it open.

"I'll write after I'm settled," my wife said. "I think I will, anyway. But first things first. We'll have to see."

"Now you're talking," the deputy said. "Keep all lines of

communication open. Good luck, pardee," the deputy said to me. Then he went over to his car and got in.

The pick-up made a wide, slow turn with the trailer across the lawn. One of the horses whinnied. The last image I have of my wife was when a match flared in the cab of the pick-up, and I saw her lean over with a cigarette to accept the light the rancher was offering. Her hands were cupped around the hand that held the match. The deputy waited until the pick-up and trailer had gone past him and then he swung his car around, slipping in the wet grass until he found purchase on the driveway, throwing gravel from under his tyres. As he headed for the road, he tooted his horn. *Tooted.* Historians should use more words like "tooted" or "beeped" or "blasted" – especially at serious moments such as after a massacre or when an awful occurrence has cast a pall on the future of an entire nation. That's when a word like "tooted" is necessary, is gold in a brass age.

I'd like to say it was at this moment, as I stood in the fog watching her drive off, that I remembered a black-and-white photograph of my wife holding her wedding bouquet. She was eighteen years old – *a mere girl,* her mother had shouted at me only a month before the wedding. A few minutes before the photo, she'd got married. She's smiling. She's just finished, or is just about to begin, laughing. In either case, her mouth is open in amazed happiness as she looks into the camera. She is three months pregnant, though the camera doesn't show that, of course. But what if she *is* pregnant? So what? Wasn't everybody pregnant in those days? She's happy, in any case. I was happy, too – I know I was. We were both happy. I'm not in that particular picture, but I was close – only a few steps away, as I remember, shaking hands with someone offering me good wishes. My wife knew Latin and German and chemistry and physics and history and

Shakespeare and all those other things they teach you in private school. She knew how to properly hold a teacup. She also knew how to cook and to make love. She was a prize.

But I found this photograph, along with several others, a few days after the horse business, when I was going through my wife's belongings, trying to see what I could throw out and what I should keep. I was packing to move, and I looked at the photograph for a minute and then I threw it away. I was ruthless. I told myself I didn't care. Why should I care?

If I know anything – and I do – if I know the slightest thing about human nature, I know she won't be able to live without me. She'll come back to me. And soon. Let it be soon.

No, I don't know anything about anything, and I never did. She's gone for good. She is. I can feel it. Gone and never coming back. Period. Not ever. I won't see her again, unless we run into each other on the street somewhere.

There's still the question of the handwriting. That's a bewilderment. But the handwriting business isn't the important thing, of course. How could it be after the consequences of the letter? Not the letter itself but the things I can't forget that were *in* the letter. No, the letter is not paramount at all – there's far more to this than somebody's handwriting. The "far more" has to do with subtle things. It could be said, for instance, that to take a wife is to take a history. And if that's so, then I understand that I'm outside history now – like horses and fog. Or you could say that my history has left me. Or that I'm having to go on *without history*. Or that history will now have to do without me – unless my wife writes more letters, or tells a friend who keeps a diary, say. Then, years later, someone can look back on this time, interpret it according to the record, its scraps and tirades, its silences and innuendoes. That's when it dawns on me that autobiography is the poor man's history. And that I am saying goodbye to history. Goodbye, my darling.

Errand

Chekhov. On the evening of 22 March 1897, he went to dinner in Moscow with his friend and confidant Alexei Suvorin. This Suvorin was a very rich newspaper and book publisher, a reactionary, a self-made man whose father was a private at the battle of Borodino. Like Chekhov, he was the grandson of a serf. They had that in common: each had peasant's blood in his veins. Otherwise, politically and temperamentally, they were miles apart. Nevertheless, Suvorin was one of Chekhov's few intimates, and Chekhov enjoyed his company.

Naturally, they went to the best restaurant in the city, a former town house called the Hermitage – a place where it could take hours, half the night even, to get through a ten-course meal that would, of course, include several wines, liqueurs, and coffee. Chekhov was impeccably dressed, as always – a dark suit and waistcoat, his usual pince-nez. He looked that night very much as he looks in the photographs taken of him during this period. He was relaxed, jovial. He shook hands with the maître d', and with a glance took in the large dining room. It was brilliantly illuminated by ornate chandeliers, the tables occupied by elegantly dressed men and women. Waiters came and went ceaselessly. He had just been seated across the table from Suvorin when suddenly, without warning, blood began gushing from his mouth. Suvorin and two waiters helped him to the gentlemen's room and tried to stanch the flow of blood with ice packs. Suvorin saw him back to his own hotel and had a bed prepared for Chekhov in one of the rooms of the suite. Later, after another haemorrhage, Chekhov allowed himself to be moved to a clinic that specialized in the treatment of tuberculosis and related respiratory infections. When Suvorin visited him there, Chekhov apologized for the "scandal" at the restaurant three nights earlier but continued to insist there was nothing seriously wrong. "He laughed and jested as usual," Suvorin noted in his diary, "while spitting blood into a large vessel."

Maria Chekhov, his younger sister, visited Chekhov in the clinic during the last days of March. The weather was miserable; a sleet storm was in progress, and frozen heaps of snow lay everywhere. It was hard for her to wave down a carriage to take her to the hospital. By the time she arrived she was filled with dread and anxiety.

"Anton Pavlovich lay on his back," Maria wrote in her *Memoirs*. "He was not allowed to speak. After greeting him, I went over to the table to hide my emotions." There, among bottles of champagne, jars of caviar, bouquets of flowers from well-wishers, she saw something that terrified her: a freehand drawing, obviously done by a specialist in these matters, of Chekhov's lungs. It was the kind of sketch a doctor often makes in order to show his patient what he thinks is taking place. The lungs were outlined in blue, but the upper parts were filled in with red. "I realized they were diseased," Maria wrote.

Leo Tolstoy was another visitor. The hospital staff were awed to find themselves in the presence of the country's greatest writer. The most famous man in Russia? Of course they had to let him in to see Chekhov, even though "nonessential" visitors were forbidden. With much obsequiousness on the part of the nurses and resident doctors, the bearded, fierce-looking old man was shown into Chekhov's room.

Despite his low opinion of Chekhov's abilities as a playwright (Tolstoy felt the plays were static and lacking in any moral vision. "Where do your characters take you?" he once demanded of Chekhov. "From the sofa to the junk room and back."), Tolstoy liked Chekhov's short stories. Furthermore, and quite simply, he loved the man. He told Gorky, "What a beautiful, magnificent man: modest and quiet, like a girl. He even walks like a girl. He's simply wonderful." And Tolstoy wrote in his journal (everyone kept a journal or a diary in those days), "I am glad I love . . . Chekhov."

Tolstoy removed his woollen scarf and bearskin coat, then lowered himself into a chair next to Chekhov's bed. Never mind that Chekhov was taking medication and not permitted to talk, much less carry on a conversation. He had to listen, amazedly, as the Count began to discourse on his theories of the immortality of the soul. Concerning that visit, Chekhov later wrote, "Tolstoy assumes that all of us (humans and animals alike) will live on in a principle (such as reason or love) the essence and goals of which are a mystery to us . . . I have no use for that kind of immortality. I don't understand it, and Lev Nikolayevich was astonished I didn't."

Nevertheless, Chekhov was impressed with the solicitude shown by Tolstoy's visit. But, unlike Tolstoy, Chekhov didn't believe in an afterlife and never had. He didn't believe in anything that couldn't be apprehended by one or more of his five senses. And as far as his outlook on life and writing went, he once told someone that he lacked "a political, religious, and philosophical world view. I change it every month, so I'll have to limit myself to the description of how my heroes love, marry, give birth, die, and how they speak."

Earlier, before his TB was diagnosed, Chekhov had remarked, "When a peasant has consumption, he says, 'There's nothing I can do. I'll go off in the spring with the melting of the snows.'" (Chekhov himself died in the summer, during a heat wave.) But once Chekhov's own tuberculosis was discovered he continually tried to minimize the seriousness of his condition. To all appearances, it was as if he felt, right up to the end, that he might be able to throw off the disease as he would a lingering catarrh. Well into his final days, he spoke with seeming conviction of the possibility of an improvement. In fact, in a letter written shortly before his end, he went so far as to tell his sister that he was "getting fat" and felt much better now that he was in Badenweiler.

Badenweiler is a spa and resort city in the western area of the Black Forest, not far from Basel. The Vosges are visible from nearly anywhere in the city, and in those days the air was pure and invigorating. Russians had been going there for years to soak in the hot mineral baths and promenade on the boulevards. In June 1904, Chekhov went there to die.

Earlier that month, he'd made a difficult journey by train from Moscow to Berlin. He travelled with his wife, the actress Olga Knipper, a woman he'd met in 1898 during rehearsals for *The Seagull*. Her contemporaries describe her as an excellent actress. She was talented, pretty, and almost ten years younger than the playwright. Chekhov had been immediately attracted to her, but was slow to act on his feelings. As always, he preferred a flirtation to marriage. Finally, after a three-year courtship involving many separations, letters, and the inevitable misunderstandings, they were married, in a private ceremony in Moscow, on 25 May 1901. Chekhov was enormously happy. He called Olga his "pony", and sometimes "dog" or "puppy". He was also fond of addressing her as "little turkey" or simply as "my joy".

In Berlin, Chekhov consulted with a renowned specialist in pulmonary disorders, a Dr Karl Ewald. But, according to an eyewitness, after the doctor examined Chekhov he threw up his hands and left the room without a word. Chekhov was too far gone for help: this Dr Ewald was furious with himself for not being able to work miracles, and with Chekhov for being so ill.

A Russian journalist happened to visit the Chekhovs at their hotel and sent back this dispatch to his editor: "Chekhov's days are numbered. He seems mortally ill, is terribly thin, coughs all the time, gasps for breath at the slightest movement, and is running a high temperature." This same journalist saw the Chekhovs off at Potsdam Station when they boarded their train for Badenweiler. According to his account, "Chekhov had trouble making his way up the small staircase at the station. He had to sit down for several minutes to catch his breath." In fact, it was painful for Chekhov to move: his legs ached continually and his insides hurt. The disease had attacked his intestines and spinal cord. At this point he had less than a month to live. When Chekhov spoke of his condition now, it was, according to Olga, "with an almost reckless indifference".

Dr Schwöhrer was one of the many Badenweiler physicians who earned a good living by treating the well-to-do who came to the spa seeking relief from various maladies. Some of his patients were ill and infirm, others simply old and hypochondriacal. But Chekhov's was a special case: he was clearly beyond help and in his last days. He was also very famous. Even Dr Schwöhrer knew his name: he'd read some of Chekhov's stories in a German magazine. When he examined the writer early in June, he voiced his appreciation of Chekhov's art but kept his medical opinions to himself. Instead, he prescribed a diet of cocoa, oatmeal drenched in butter, and strawberry tea. This last was supposed to help Chekhov sleep at night.

On 13 June, less than three weeks before he died, Chekhov wrote a letter to his mother in which he told her his health was on the mend. In it he said, "It's likely that I'll be completely cured in a week." Who knows why he said this? What could he have been thinking? He was a doctor himself, and he knew better. He was dying, it was as simple and as unavoidable as that. Nevertheless, he sat out on the balcony of his hotel room and read railway timetables. He asked for information on sailings of boats bound for Odessa from Marseilles. But he *knew*. At this stage he had to have known. Yet in one of the last letters he ever wrote he told his sister he was growing stronger by the day.

He no longer had any appetite for literary work, and hadn't for a long time. In fact, he had very nearly failed to complete *The Cherry Orchard* the year before. Writing that play was the hardest thing he'd ever done in his life. Towards the end, he was able to manage only six or seven lines a day. "I've started losing heart," he wrote Olga. "I feel I'm finished as a writer, and every sentence strikes me as worthless and of no use whatever." But he didn't stop. He finished his play in October 1903. It was the last thing he ever wrote, except for letters and a few entries in his notebook.

A little after midnight on 2 July 1904, Olga sent someone to fetch Dr Schwöhrer. It was an emergency: Chekhov was delirious. Two young Russians on holiday happened to have the adjacent room, and Olga hurried next door to explain what was happening. One of the youths was in his bed asleep, but the other was still awake, smoking and reading. He left the hotel at a run to find Dr Schwöhrer. "I can still hear the sound of the gravel under his shoes in the silence of that stifling July night," Olga wrote later on in her memoirs. Chekhov was hallucinating, talking about sailors, and there were snatches of something about the Japanese. "You don't put ice on an empty stomach," he said when she tried to place an ice pack on his chest.

Dr Schwöhrer arrived and unpacked his bag, all the while keeping his gaze fastened on Chekhov, who lay gasping in the bed. The sick man's pupils were dilated and his temples glistened with sweat. Dr Schwöhrer's face didn't register anything. He was not an emotional man, but he knew Chekhov's end was near. Still, he was a doctor, sworn to do his utmost, and Chekhov held on to life, however tenuously. Dr Schwöhrer prepared a hypodermic and administered an injection of camphor, something that was supposed to speed up the heart. But the injection didn't help – nothing, of course, could have helped. Nevertheless, the doctor made known to Olga his intention of sending for oxygen. Suddenly, Chekhov roused himself, became lucid, and said quietly, "What's the use? Before it arrives I'll be a corpse."

Dr Schwöhrer pulled on his big moustache and stared at Chekhov. The writer's cheeks were sunken and grey, his complexion waxen; his breath was raspy. Dr Schwöhrer knew the time could be reckoned in minutes. Without a word, without conferring with Olga, he went over to an alcove where there was a telephone on the wall. He read the instructions for using the device. If he activated it by holding his finger on a button and turning a handle on the side of the phone, he could reach the lower regions of the hotel – the kitchen. He picked up the receiver, held it to his ear, and did as the instructions told him. When someone finally answered, Dr Schwöhrer ordered a bottle of the hotel's best champagne. "How many glasses?" he was asked. "Three glasses!" the doctor shouted into the mouthpiece. "And hurry, do you hear?" It was one of those rare moments of inspiration that can easily enough be overlooked later on, because the action is so entirely appropriate it seems inevitable.

The champagne was brought to the door by a tired-looking young man whose blond hair was standing up. The trousers of his uniform were wrinkled, the creases gone, and in his haste he'd missed a loop while buttoning his jacket. His appearance was that of someone who'd been resting (slumped in a chair, say, dozing a little), when off in the distance the phone had clamoured in the early-morning hours – great God in Heaven! – and the next thing he knew he was being shaken awake by a superior and told to deliver a bottle of Moët to Room 211. "And hurry, do you hear?"

The young man entered the room carrying a silver ice bucket with the champagne in it and a silver tray with three cut-crystal glasses. He found a place on the table for the bucket and glasses, all the while craning his neck, trying to see into the other room, where someone panted ferociously for breath. It was a dreadful, harrowing sound, and the young man lowered his chin into his collar and turned away as the ratchety breathing worsened. Forgetting himself, he stared out the open window towards the darkened city. Then this big imposing man with a thick moustache pressed some coins into his hand – a large tip, by the feel of it – and suddenly the young man saw the door open. He took some steps and found himself on the landing, where he opened his hand and looked at the coins in amazement.

Methodically, the way he did everything, the doctor went about the business of working the cork out of the bottle. He did it in such a way as to minimize, as much as possible, the festive explosion. He poured three glasses and, out of habit, pushed the cork back into the neck of the bottle. He then took the glasses of champagne over to the bed. Olga momentarily released her grip on Chekhov's hand – a hand, she said later, that burned her fingers. She arranged another pillow behind his head. Then she put the cool glass of champagne against Chekhov's palm and made sure his fingers closed around the stem. They exchanged looks – Chekhov, Olga, Dr Schwöhrer. They didn't touch glasses. There was no toast. What on earth was there to drink to? To death? Chekhov summoned his remaining strength and said, "It's been so long since I've had champagne." He brought the glass to his lips and drank. In a minute or two Olga took the empty glass from his hand and set it on the nightstand. Then Chekhov turned on to his side. He closed his eyes and sighed. A minute later, his breathing stopped.

Dr Schwöhrer picked up Chekhov's hand from the bed-sheet. He held his fingers to Chekhov's wrist and drew a gold watch from his vest pocket, opening the lid of the watch as he did so. The second hand on the watch moved slowly, very slowly. He let it move around the face of the watch three times while he waited for signs of a pulse. It was three o'clock in the morning and still sultry in the room. Baden-weiler was in the grip of its worst heat wave in years. All the windows in both rooms stood open, but there was no sign of a breeze. A large, black-winged moth flew through a window and banged wildly against the electric lamp. Dr Schwöhrer let go of Chekhov's wrist. "It's over," he said. He closed the lid of his watch and returned it to his vest pocket.

At once Olga dried her eyes and set about composing herself. She thanked the doctor for coming. He asked if she wanted some medication – laudanum, perhaps, or a few drops of valerian. She shook her head. She did have one request, though: before the authorities were notified and the news-papers found out, before the time came when Chekhov was no longer in her keeping, she wanted to be alone with him for a while. Could the doctor help with this? Could he withhold, for a while anyway, news of what had just occurred?

Dr Schwöhrer stroked his moustache with the back of a finger. Why not? After all, what difference would it make to anyone whether this matter became known now or a few hours from now? The only detail that remained was to fill out a death certificate, and this could be done at his office later in the morning, after he'd slept a few hours. Dr Schwöhrer nodded his agreement and prepared to leave. He murmured a few words of condolence. Olga inclined her head. "An honour," Dr Schwöhrer said. He picked up his bag and left the room and, for that matter, history.

It was at this moment that the cork popped out of the champagne bottle; foam spilled down on to the table. Olga went back to Chekhov's bedside. She sat on a footstool, holding his hand, from time to time stroking his face. "There were no human voices, no everyday sounds," she wrote. "There was only beauty, peace, and the grandeur of death."

She stayed with Chekhov until daybreak, when thrushes began to call from the garden below. Then came the sound of tables and chairs being moved about down there. Before long, voices carried up to her. It was then a knock sounded at the door. Of course she thought it must be an official of some sort – the medical examiner, say, or someone from the police who had questions to ask and forms for her to fill out, or maybe, just maybe, it could be Dr Schwöhrer returning with a mortician to render assistance in embalming and transporting Chekhov's remains back to Russia.

But, instead, it was the same blond young man who'd brought the champagne a few hours earlier. This time, however, his uniform trousers were neatly pressed, with stiff creases in front, and every button on his snug green jacket was fastened. He seemed quite another person. Not only was he wide awake but his plump cheeks were smooth-shaven, his hair was in place, and he appeared anxious to please. He was holding a porcelain vase with three long-stemmed yellow roses. He presented these to Olga with a smart click of his heels. She stepped back and let him into the room. He was there, he said, to collect the glasses, ice bucket, and tray, yes. But he also wanted to say that, because of the extreme heat, breakfast would be served in the garden this morning. He hoped this weather wasn't too bothersome; he apologized for it.

The woman seemed distracted. While he talked, she turned her eyes away and looked down at something in the carpet. She crossed her arms and held her elbows. Meanwhile, still holding his vase, waiting for a sign, the young man took in the details of the room. Bright sunlight flooded through the open windows. The room was tidy and seemed undisturbed, almost untouched. No garments were flung over chairs, no shoes, stockings, braces, or stays were in evidence, no open suitcases. In short, there was no clutter, nothing but the usual heavy pieces of hotel-room furniture. Then, because the woman was still looking down, he looked down, too, and at once spied a cork near the toe of his shoe. The woman did not see it – she was looking somewhere else. The young man wanted to bend over and pick up the cork, but he was still holding the roses and was afraid of seeming to intrude even more by drawing any further attention to himself. Reluctantly, he left the cork where it was and raised his eyes. Everything was in order except for the uncorked, half-empty bottle of champagne that stood alongside two crystal glasses over on the little table. He cast his gaze about once more. Through an open door he saw that the third glass was in the bedroom, on the nightstand. But someone still occupied the bed! He couldn't see a face, but the figure under the covers lay perfectly motionless and quiet. He noted the figure and looked elsewhere. Then, for a reason he couldn't understand, a feeling of uneasiness took hold of him. He cleared his throat and moved his weight to the other leg. The woman still didn't look up or break her silence. The young man felt his cheeks grow warm. It occurred to him, quite without his having thought it through, that he should perhaps suggest an alternative to breakfast in the garden. He coughed, hoping to focus the woman's attention, but she didn't look at him. The distinguished foreign guests could, he said, take breakfast in their rooms this morning if they wished. The young man (his name hasn't survived, and it's likely he perished in the Great

War) said he would be happy to bring up a tray. Two trays, he added, glancing uncertainly once again in the direction of the bedroom.

He fell silent and ran a finger around the inside of his collar. He didn't understand. He wasn't even sure the woman had been listening. He didn't know what else to do now; he was still holding the vase. The sweet odour of the roses filled his nostrils and inexplicably caused a pang of regret. The entire time he'd been waiting, the woman had apparently been lost in thought. It was as if all the while he'd been standing there, talking, shifting his weight, holding his flowers, she had been someplace else, somewhere far from Badenweiler. But now she came back to herself, and her face assumed another expression. She raised her eyes, looked at him, and then shook her head. She seemed to be struggling to understand what on earth this young man could be doing there in the room holding a vase with three yellow roses. Flowers? She hadn't ordered flowers.

The moment passed. She went over to her handbag and scooped up some coins. She drew out a number of banknotes as well. The young man touched his lips with his tongue; another large tip was forthcoming, but for what? What did she want him to do? He'd never before waited on such guests. He cleared his throat once more.

No breakfast, the woman said. Not yet, at any rate. Breakfast wasn't the important thing this morning. She required something else. She needed him to go out and bring back a mortician. Did he understand her? Herr Chekhov was dead, you see. *Comprenez-vous?* Young man? Anton Chekhov was dead. Now listen carefully to me, she said. She wanted him to go downstairs and ask someone at the front desk where he could go to find the most respected mortician in the city. Someone reliable, who took great pains in his work and whose manner was appropriately reserved. A mortician, in short, worthy of a great artist. Here, she said, and pressed the money on him. Tell them downstairs that I have specifically requested you to perform this duty for me. Are you listening? Do you understand what I'm saying to you?

The young man grappled to take in what she was saying. He chose not to look again in the direction of the other room. He had sensed that something was not right. He became aware of his heart beating rapidly under his jacket and he felt perspiration break out on his forehead. He didn't know where he should turn his eyes. He wanted to put the vase down.

Please do this for me, the woman said. I'll remember you with gratitude. Tell them downstairs that I insist. Say that. But don't call any unnecessary attention to yourself or to the situation. Just say that this is necessary, that I request it – and that's all. Do you hear me? Nod if you understand. Above all, don't raise an alarm. Everything else, all the rest, the commotion – that'll come soon enough. The worst is over. Do we understand each other?

The young man's face had grown pale. He stood rigid, clasping the vase. He managed to nod his head.

After securing permission to leave the hotel he was to proceed quietly and resolutely, though without any unbecoming haste, to the mortician's. He was to behave exactly as if he were engaged on a very important errand, nothing more. He *was* engaged on an important errand, she said. And if it would help keep his movements purposeful he should imagine himself as someone moving down the busy sidewalk carrying in his arms a porcelain vase of roses that he had to deliver to an important man. (She spoke quietly, almost confidentially, as if to a relative or a friend.) He could even tell himself that the man he was going to see was expecting him, was perhaps impatient for him to arrive with his flowers. Nevertheless, the young man was not to become excited and run, or otherwise break his stride. Remember the vase he was carrying! He was to walk briskly, comporting himself at all times in as dignified a manner as possible. He should keep walking until he came to the mortician's house and stood before the door. He would then raise the brass knocker and let it fall, once, twice, three times. In a minute the mortician himself would answer.

This mortician would be in his forties, no doubt, or maybe early fifties – bald, solidly built, wearing steel-frame spectacles set very low on his nose. He would be modest, unassuming, a man who would ask only the most direct and necessary questions. An apron. Probably he would be wearing an apron. He might even be wiping his hands on a dark towel while he listened to what was being said. There'd be a faint whiff of formaldehyde on his clothes. But it was all right, and the young man shouldn't worry. He was nearly a grown-up now and shouldn't be frightened or repelled by any of this. The mortician would hear him out. He was a man of restraint and bearing, this mortician, someone who could help allay people's fears in this situation, not increase them. Long ago he'd acquainted himself with death in all its various guises and forms; death held no surprises for him any longer, no hidden secrets. It was this man whose services were required this morning.

The mortician takes the vase of roses. Only once while the young man is speaking does the mortician betray the least flicker of interest, or indicate that he's heard anything out of the ordinary. But the one time the young man mentions the name of the deceased, the mortician's eyebrows rise just a little. Chekhov, you say? Just a minute, and I'll be with you.

Do you understand what I'm saying, Olga said to the young man. Leave the glasses. Don't worry about them. Forget about crystal wineglasses and such. Leave the room as it is. Everything is ready now. We're ready. Will you go?

But at that moment the young man was thinking of the cork still resting near the toe of his shoe. To retrieve it he would have to bend over, still gripping the vase. He would do this. He leaned over. Without looking down, he reached out and closed it into his hand.